A HUSBAND NEVER LIES

A Psychological Thriller

James Caine

Twisted Thriller Books

PROLOGUE

Every person who's married will tell you that marriage has its ups and downs. You can go from a dark place where you want to wring your partner's neck for the dumbest reasons to feeling like it's the beginning of your relationship all over again. You'll feel those butterflies in your stomach when they touch you. A feeling of yearning with a simple stare from them.

Kevin and I are due our better times.

We've been going through our valley for some time, and we've only been married for nearly two years. In fact, our anniversary is coming up soon.

Kevin shuffles in the bedsheets, rolling over to his side towards me. I take in how gorgeous he is. I truly have a handsome husband. He was always in good shape, but he put on a little weight during our first year of marriage.

I thought it was more comfort weight gain. He was no longer looking for a partner. He found his forever mate with me. He was very lean on our wedding night. He's much more active than I am. He loves doing anything outside. Fishing, hunting, hiking, skiing, he loves it all. I was impressed when he showed me a photo of him mountain climbing.

I think when you find a partner, you compliment each other and take on some of the other's personality traits. I tamed him to be a little less active. He got me to do more outdoor activities.

He's lost his comfort weight now. Actually, he's even thinner now than before we were married. He got into fasting and rarely eats breakfast with me now. I feel like such a fatso compared to him when I'm scarfing down pancakes, cereal, or any kind of unhealthy carb I can find in the morning while he drinks his coffee, black with no sugar or milk.

"Jo," he always says, "fast with me. We could do it together."

Fasting isn't my thing, though. I have a very unhealthy relationship with food. I've always known it, but it's starting to catch up with me in negative ways.

Although my husband is looking better than ever, I hate how insecure it makes me feel. While he's gotten better-looking, by most standards, I've let myself go. I remind myself he doesn't care about that. He loves me. He tells me this all the time.

Late last night, he showed me he meant those words. The sex was passionate. It was amazing. Another skill Kevin has. He has a way of reading my body like a roadmap, knowing which direction to take and when and how fast to drive.

It's nearly five in the morning, and as I lie in bed with my husband, I reflect on how much I love him. The adventure my life has taken since we met. The love he brought into my life.

He's sleeping shirtless. He always does, but with his recent weight loss and workouts, I can see a partial four pack on his lower abdomen peeking out, teasing me. The sight of his body makes my mind wander in not-so-innocent ways, and I wonder what would happen if I woke him. I'd love him to read my roadmap again.

He has to work today, though, and so do I. But if I wake him up a few hours earlier, he likely won't be upset.

Isn't sex better than starting your day with a cup of coffee?

"Hey," I whisper to him. I caress the side of his face, letting my hand follow his neck, down to his chest. My hand finds a home on his blossoming abs, and I feel the slight ridge of his abdomen muscles. "Are you awake?"

He lets out a puff of air and for a moment I wait for his gorgeous blue eyes to lock onto mine. I anticipate his devilish smile meeting my own with the same intentions.

"Josie," he whispers. His face twitches.

"Morning," I say to him as I caress his body more, my hands lowering to find him as excited as I hoped he would be.

My hopes for an intimate morning turn sour as he turns to the other side, facing the wall, making weird noises—an odd combination of grumbling and snoring.

Perfect.

I let out a sigh. I want my husband, but not badly enough to start shaking him violently until he wakes up.

Defeated, I stare at the ceiling again. The fan hypnotizes my eyes shut, dazing me back to a sleepy state until I catch a smiling face I recognize beside me. A photo from our wedding day. I was smiling wide for the picture as Kevin dipped me in my wedding dress on the dancefloor. It's hard to imagine that it's nearly been two years with Kevin. Not too long ago, I said, "I do," and became Josie McNeil.

Suddenly, I get another urge. I slip out of the bedsheets and make my way to the bathroom connected to our bedroom. As I do, Kevin makes another snorting sound and contorts his face. I hope that he'll open his eyes and we'll be game for a fun morning, but he stops moving and continues breathing heavily.

Suddenly, a buzzing sound from the nightstand beside him catches my attention. I look down and his cell vibrates again. The screen lights up with a text message.

Kevin's knocked out, unaware someone is trying to reach him. Someone getting his attention at five in the morning?

Who could be messaging him this early? Maybe his work needs him to come in early. Kev's been putting in the hours lately. His research project is already past its deadline. Kev's the lead researcher of his group at Marada Pharmaceuticals, where they're testing a new medication to lower cholesterol.

Worried that it's some type of work emergency, I pick up his cell phone. If it's a work issue, I'll wake up my peaceful, resting husband. Otherwise, whoever this is can wait until a much more appropriate time to respond.

I look at the cell phone screen and read the message. My mouth drops as I do, wondering what I'm seeing. What does it mean? Who sent it? The number is a bunch of random digits and isn't a saved contact on his phone.

I look at my husband lying on the bed, trying to

figure this out. Is this some kind of nightmare? Am I still dreaming.

"I had fun last night. Let's do that again sometime." A stupid winking face emoji is beside the text.

I read the message for a third time before the screen goes dark. I grip his phone sternly, my mouth widening, and I try to make sense of it.

Had fun last night? Wasn't he out with his work colleagues before coming home? That's what he told me. I click on the side button of his phone and look at the message again to ensure I'm not going crazy.

"I had fun last night." I stop reading as I get more upset. I can see the winking emoji in my head mocking me. I look down at my sleeping husband as I try to rationalize the message.

Who the fu—

CHAPTER 1

Kevin got up and did his usual morning routine. I heard him whistle as he shaved and hummed some song in the shower. I lay in bed, curled up in a ball, feeling paralyzed. Unable to move my limbs in any way besides distorting myself like a baby in its crib.

Who texted Kev at five in the morning? What did they mean that they had a fun time last night? What could that possibly be about? My brain is already filling in the blanks with the obvious.

He slept with someone. Did he hook up with some floozy at the bar where he and his coworkers went? He's been going out more often and spending less time with me. It was starting to bother me to the point that I told him I needed to spend more quality time with him. I was worried he was actively ignoring me at home.

When I told him how I felt, he told me he wasn't trying to hurt my feelings. Work's been tough, he explained. His team missed an important deadline and they've been working like mad to finish the project.

As he explained himself, I felt bad for even questioning him like I'm some clingy wife. He warned me ahead of time that the next few weeks were going to be hectic. And yet, here we are. His life is hectic as expected and he barely has time for anything, but I still get upset.

After we made love last night, I felt at peace. I felt connected to Kev again. Perhaps his words didn't reassure me that everything was okay, but his body did.

I hear pawing at the door. Q has been waiting patiently for me to open the bedroom door for her. Kev had one rule when we got a cat: she doesn't sleep on the bed. He has trouble sleeping and an animal walking around him as he tries to rest wouldn't help.

When I open the bedroom door, Q brushes against my leg and her cute face looks up at me with anticipation. I know what she wants, and I could use a snuggle this morning.

I pick her up and lay on the bed, petting her. I wanted to adopt a cat from an animal rescue, but Kevin insisted on getting a kitten. When we went to a pet store, there was a litter of kittens to choose from. All of them had the cutest white kitty fur peppered with black spots.

Beside them, in one of the upper cages, was an older cat. There was no name on her cage, like some of the other cats that surrounded her. I was told later that this was because the staff didn't have a chance to put up her information. All it said on hers was "Q", which was her cage letter.

For whatever reason, that got to my heartstrings. I imagined other people coming to the store to find a new pet and picking one of the kittens immediately. Who wouldn't? I could see others choosing some of the older cats too.

When I looked at Q that first day, I imagined nobody choosing her. I couldn't stand the thought. Kev agreed to take her to a small room the staff uses to see if an animal is a good fit for them. Kevin and I sat in two chairs as we waited for staff to bring her in. I fell in love with Q immediately when she was brought to us and she jumped on my lap.

The staff told me that Q wasn't her name, but I told them I didn't want to know her real one. She was a rescue that the store took in. The name that was given to her by the people who gave her away wasn't needed anymore.

Now she could have a new life as Q. Also known as Ms. Q, or Cutie Q, or whatever name I come up with when I'm around her. Usually when I pet her, whatever problems I have don't seem as big, but this morning even Q isn't helping.

Kev turns off the shower. I hear him step out, humming at a low murmur whatever song's stuck on his mind.

Who else was at the bar with him last night? His work friends for sure, but I can't help but wonder if that includes Stacy Wingham. She's a slender, pretty blond girl who always manages to have on the tightest outfits, showcasing her best pair of assets for the world to see.

Anybody would notice her, and I'm sure Kev has too. They work closely together. Kev's the team lead but she's his assistant leader. I joked to him once that she's his *work wife*. He laughed it off but didn't try to refute it. I had hoped he would have said something like, "No, Jo, stop being jealous." Instead, he just laughed.

"I had fun last night. Let's do that again sometime."

Was that Stacy who messaged him? If it was, perhaps it's all innocent. Maybe the text should be taken at face value. They went out last night to the bar, together with co-workers and "had fun". Drank and joked amongst friends. Let off some steam after a busy day at work.

But she's texting him at five in the morning?

That doesn't make sense. Did she wake up, think of

my husband and message him? That's assuming it's her. I know a few of the other men who work with him. I met a coworker, a guy named James. He picked Kev up from home one night to go out. There's also another guy named Adam that Kev talks frequently about.

Both don't exactly sound like people who would be texting my husband at five in the morning. Do guys text each other nice things like that after a night out at the bar? I assumed they sat around talking about boobs all night as they drank.

That makes me think of Stacy Wingham and her assets again.

Ugh. I know I'm spiraling, and I feel like there's nothing I can do about it. At some point, Kevin got out of bed and cleared the message from his phone before going into the bathroom. That means he saw the message. It's no longer on his cell screen.

Did he respond? I was too busy being stuck in my head about what's happening to notice.

Kev walks into the room, drying his hair with a towel. His damp hair clings to his forehead, and the sharp, clean scent of his aftershave lingers in the air as he passes.

"Morning," he says with a smile.

Just ask him, a voice says inside me. I don't listen though. I've made the mistake of questioning him before. I snooped on his phone in the past. There was a time when we weren't intimate for several months and I worried that meant there was someone else. I felt certain there was. I swiped his phone one night while he was asleep and went into the living room downstairs. Back then, I knew his password. I spent over an hour going through any conversation I could find but discovered nothing that suggested my husband was up to no good.

I put the cell back on the nightstand. He went about his day not knowing I had snooped. I easily could have gotten away with it, only I felt rotten inside. Sure, he had no clue what I did, but the guilt consumed me. I was becoming a woman I never thought I'd be. The jealous kind. A husband and wife need to trust each other. Without trust, the foundation of your whole relationship is built on shaky grounds.

I fessed up and told Kev that I looked on his phone and why. I'm not sure how I expected him to react. It was intense.

Anger almost on the verge of rage was his response. He was devastated that I broke his privacy. He told me if I ever did that again, he'd leave me. I thought that was a severe reaction.

I thought coming clean to him would make me feel better, but it made everything worse. So much for a gut feeling. He no longer has the same password now. I checked before attempting to go back to sleep. I just needed to know who the person was who messaged him.

I'll learn from my mistakes though. This time I won't tell him what I tried to do.

Kev laughs at me. "What's the matter?" he asks. "You didn't sleep good last night?" He leans close to me and pets Q fiercely on the head.

If only he knew the truth. If only I could find out without pissing him off again.

"I tossed and turned a lot," I say. "You got up earlier today."

He nods. "I have to get to work. We're under a lot of pressure to finish the project." He opens the walk-in closet and steps inside, browsing through his wardrobe. He finally picks out a pair of dark grey chinos and a light blue button-up.

"How was the bar last night?" I ask.

He tosses the shirt around his back and starts to button it up. "Good," he says curtly.

"You went to that sports bar by your work, right?" I ask. He just nods in response. "Who all went?"

He smirks at me and glances down, putting on the last button. "I told you last night when I got home. The usual guys. James and Adam and one of the new temp guys they hired."

"That's fun," I say, not getting the information I need. I want to yell at him. Who texted you and why did they have "fun" last night? "Stacy didn't go?" I examine his face like a police detective hoping for a micro expression to give away the truth.

He shakes his head at first. "Or wait, yeah, she did, but she came late."

Aha! So, she was there. "Nobody else showed up?" As I ask, I continue to pet Q but realize I'm being a little rough.

He puts on his pants and wraps a belt through the knots on his chinos. "What's with the interview this morning?" He lets out a laugh. "We just had beers and wings. The usual." Before I can ask more, he walks up to me and kisses the side of my cheek. "Got to leave early, love," he says, pulling back immediately and grabbing a tie from the closet. He waves at me as he leaves the room.

I sit back on the bed, trying to wrap my head around everything, when suddenly Kev pops his head back into the room. "By the way, I had a lot of fun last night." He brandishes a quick smile before leaving.

CHAPTER 2

My morning has been me continuously spiraling out of control. All I can think about is who may have texted Kev so early today.

I keep imagining the woman who he works with, Stacy. Or maybe it's some random woman he met. One thing's for certain: it can't be another man who wrote him that, and with that winking emoji.

There are moments where I tell myself I'm catastrophizing the text message. It's not a big deal. I've doubted Kevin before and look what that brought me. It only gave me more headaches and more issues with our marriage. It got to a point that I asked him to join couples' counseling with me.

"No," was his quick and concise response. "I don't need therapy."

Of course, he mentioned I should go. Apparently, I was the only one who needs help. He wasn't wrong. What we've been through the past year has been difficult to manage at times. Thankfully, my friends and Kev helped me get through it.

It still has its scars though. I look down at my body, the outline of my stomach visible through my pajama shirt that's a little too tight for me. I'm too stubborn to buy new clothes.

I try to take my mind off what happened and get ready for work myself. I work in northeast Calgary but live in the southwest part of the city. I'll likely be late. Not a good time to be late to a job where cuts are on the horizon. Of course, I had to choose a customer-service job where a robot may take over my career in a few short years.

Why couldn't I have been a plumber? Something that artificial intelligence won't be able to do for companies at a fraction of the cost of hiring real humans. It's all the employees at Nexen Power talk about lately.

There were talks around the cubicles of the higher-ups having closed-door meetings speaking with AI companies. Gossip spread that it would only be an AI phone call-taker. An AI to handle the initial call to figure out which department the caller needed to be transferred to. I'm sure that's how it starts.

Great. Now I've moved on from catastrophizing about my marriage to my job. It feels like I'll have nothing left in my life at this point.

I contemplate calling in sick. I haven't taken many sick days this year. Last year, I did have a short leave after what happened, but everyone understood.

I should have taken more time off. I should just quit my job before a robot takes it over. The bots can have my crappy work.

Kevin told me I could go back to school if I wanted. Find a career more rewarding. I'm not sure why I didn't take him up on the opportunity. At the time, we were doing better financially. Kev says now that the deadline for his research is already overdue, his company is out of a bonus they were promised.

Now's not the best time to approach him about

quitting.

I think about Kev. The same husband who was encouraging me to find what I want in life is the same man I think is cheating on me now? Impossible. This must all be a misunderstanding.

I skip a shower, realizing there's no way for me to have one and get to work on time. I quickly change into my work clothes. Nothing fancy, just something that meets Nexen's "a step above casual" dress code. My white blouse and dark jeans work well.

What about Mary?

The thought of her stops me in my tracks. I haven't thought of Mary Halbec for a long time. She's Kev's ex-fiancée. He left her after he discovered she was unfaithful. They were together for eight years. After they broke up, she wouldn't stop harassing him. She was always trying to get him to come out for a coffee or a beer.

She couldn't understand why they couldn't be friends. Kev wanted nothing to do with her, though. That seemed to only make things worse. The more he ignored her, the more insane she became.

They had been broken up for over six months by the time I came into the picture. I was surprised that you could meet a decent man on a dating website. I was pretty close to giving up before I met Kevin.

I take a deep breath, reminding myself that it likely isn't Mary who texted him. Kev never mentions her anymore. If she was to come back around, he would have said something to me.

It couldn't have been Mary. I'd be more inclined towards Stacy.

I look at the bathroom mirror and stare at myself, noticing as if for the first time all the issues about my body. My clothes are too tight. My skin looks beat up. My eyes are dull, ringed with tiredness. There's a slump in my shoulder I don't remember carrying. Every flaw feels magnified under the harsh bathroom light.

"Of course he's cheating on you," a voice says inside me. It's a dark snickering voice that pops up whenever I seem down. The voice in my head that enjoys kicking me while I'm on the floor. "You stopped taking care of yourself," the voice continues. "Why would a gorgeous man like Kevin want to continue to be with a slob like you?"

I shake my head as if I'm trying to not listen to the words that are inside my own head. Maybe Kev's right. I should have gone to therapy. The voice in my head is right. I stopped taking care of myself a long time ago. Kev's mentioned the weight gain. One time, he noticed that it had been several days since I showered and asked if I was okay.

I told him I was fine even though that was far from the truth. I'm not okay. Physically, my body is breaking down. Mentally, I feel exhausted.

It's been months though since it happened. I'm doing better now, but I still cry at times.

I don't understand how Kev can act so normal. I suppose he's trying to be my rock. The shoulder for me to cry on when I need it most.

How much longer can he be there for me without feeling like I'm his burden?

I look at the mirror again and put a hand on my tummy. A tear starts to form in my eye as I think about how quickly my life changed.

What have I become? I don't recognize the woman in the mirror anymore. This isn't who I wanted to be. A toxic wife who doesn't trust her husband. A woman who let herself go to the point that I'm having medical issues. I'm only in my thirties.

I'm supposed to be happy. I'm supposed to be enjoying my life with my handsome husband by my side.

I take a deep breath and touch my belly. I'm supposed to have a family.

CHAPTER 3

"Well, this is not appropriate!" the man yells at me. I sit in my cubicle and lower my head, wishing for the call to come to an end. "How could I have used that much electricity to get this kind of bill?"

I don't dare mention to him about the new hot tub he got. He called a month ago and the customer service rep he talked to gave him an estimate about how much extra it could add to his bill. Of course, now that he has the hot tub and his floating rate increased, he's upset. I can see on his file that the last rep recommended he go with a fixed rate for his electricity, but he refused.

Thankfully, it's a phone call and not in-person. When I started at Nexen Power, I worked at the front desk. I'll take getting yelled at over the phone over getting screamed at in person any day.

Some day, who knows, maybe I'll have a job where no one will raise their voice at me. Wouldn't that be a luxury.

"I want to talk to your manager!" the customer shouts, his voice near shrieking level.

"I can arrange for a callback, sir," I say to him. This never goes over well when I'm forced to tell them they have to wait even longer to speak to someone else after being on hold for twenty minutes to speak to me.

Sorry. I didn't design the system. I just work here. I can't exactly say that to him though. He doesn't seem to be the empathetic type who'd understand.

I imagine telling him a four-letter word and just hanging up, but life isn't that easy either. I'd get fired immediately. My boss, Mr. Dunstrow, would have me empty my cubicle by noon and a new person would be tossed into the meat grinder to take my place after a few days of training.

Maybe I'm wrong about the AI invasion. Let them have my job. If they get the level of abuse I'm used to, I'd understand why robots would want to take over the world someday.

"I've had it with you!" the man shouts. "I've been on the phone with you for nearly an hour and none of my issues are resolved and now I have to wait to speak to your boss?"

My boss is busy speaking to other "happy" customers like yourself, I think, but don't dare to say out loud. "I'm sorry that you're not happy about our call today, sir. Would you still like me to arrange for a phone call with my supervisor?"

The man grunts into the phone, yes, and hangs up immediately. I put a ticket on my system for a callback from Mr. Dunstrow.

As I take my headset off and hang it on a hook in my cubicle, I take a deep breath.

Another satisfied customer. Another perfect day at Nexen Power.

I open a drawer at my foot. Several bags of gummy candies are presented before me. After a bad call, it's not uncommon for me to have a few treats to make everything better. Somehow, the sugar high makes me forget what I'm doing with my life. Beside the candy and nearly empty bags of chips are my diabetes monitor and test strips. I've been trying to be more mindful with testing my blood sugar after meals. Snacking on the worst foods possible isn't helping.

Gestational diabetes is not supposed to be permanent. Despite the miscarriage happening months ago, my sugar levels are completely uncontrolled. At this rate, my doctor feels I'm heading towards being a type two diabetic in the near future.

Scary, but even though the idea is frightening, I still gorge like an idiot on candies and chips and whatever else makes me feel temporarily better.

After we lost our child, I took it very hard. I was early on in my second trimester when it happened. It wasn't supposed to happen.

My doctor told me it wasn't my fault. Kevin said the same. Friends and family reassured me as well. Sometimes, I wonder if I had not developed gestational diabetes, would our baby girl be in my arms by now?

"This is why he's cheating on you," the nasty voice inside me says. "This is why you don't deserve to be happy."

I shake my head and slowly slide the drawer shut. I hate myself when I get this way. I'm always self-conscious about my weight and health, but this morning, my mind's been nonstop.

When I turn my head, I see a photo of Kevin and me on our honeymoon. I stand up and stretch in my cubicle, feeling the sudden urge to run out of the building. Instead, I slowly walk outside my jail cell.

After how brutal that call was, a break is needed.

I walk down a few rows of cubicles before passing

Trey's workstation. I stare inside his cubicle. He's sitting on his computer, his back to me. Looks like he's taking a break as well. Closer to me is his cribbage board and a deck of cards on top. I smile.

Trey is one of my closest friends at Nexen. We started around the same time and even trained together back in the day. He's a funny guy who has a great personality. He also shares my love for cribbage, which is a rarity. We instantly bonded when I told him how my grandma taught me how to play cribbage when I was a little girl. Ever since, he's brought a board and a deck of cards to work, and we play now and then.

Every couple has their thing they do. Some friends get together and drink. Others maybe do hot yoga together or run. While Trey and I are just friends, despite one awkward date years ago, cribbage is definitely our thing.

Although, the thought makes me think about Kevin and me. We've been married nearly two years and I'm not exactly sure what our thing is besides our enjoyment of eating bad food together and going to fancy restaurants. I don't know how Kevin's lost weight.

Part of me wants to ask Trey for a game of cribbage, but I see he's busy on his computer. He's reading an online article from a local newspaper. The headline at the top grabs my attention as well.

"Calgary Woman Still Missing."

I've heard about this story circulating in the media.

I feel like a stalker outside his cubicle watching Trey. I hate the feeling of being watched in my cubicle. I despise it so much that I rearranged my workstation so that my back wouldn't be to someone entering my workspace. Mr. Dunstrow wasn't happy with my interior design skills and forced me to move it all back to how it's supposed to be.

I can't stand the idea of someone being able to sneak up on me.

Realizing I'm doing what I despise, I continue walking past his cubicle towards a back row of workstations.

"That's right, sir." I hear Amber Abbot's voice as she speaks to a customer as I get closer. "Not a problem," she says. I pop my head into her cubicle. She sees me from the corner of her eye and greets me with a smile, putting up a finger, gesturing for me to give her a minute. "I'm happy I'm able to help you today."

Somehow, her happy call with her customer irritates me. Why is it every caller I get seems to be pissed off with me, while Amber comes off like she's enjoying her job?

I was the one who trained Amber a few months ago. Turnover at Nexen Power is pretty high. Senior customer service representatives like Trey and I are unicorn workers. Out of the twenty in the class we trained in together years ago, we're the only two left. Despite Amber only being an employee for a short period of time, six of her colleagues in her training group have already quit.

Calgary has over a million people living in it, but I feel a large percentage of its population could have been employed at Nexen at this rate of hiring and quitting.

I really hope Amber doesn't quit though. She's one of the few at Nexen that I've become close with. Whenever there's a training class, management likes to have some of the senior employees in the training room to help out. Amber and I bonded quickly over our love for reality television shows.

"Thanks so much," Amber continues as she types in a few notes on her computer. "You have a great day as well." When she ends the call, she hangs up her headset and smiles at me.

"Morning," she says. "I came by your cube before, but you weren't in."

"Ten minutes late," I confirm. I shake my head. "What a morning."

"Bad call?" she asks. She knows me. I tend to come over to her cubicle after ending a terrible phone call, which must be why I'm in her cubicle more and more these days.

"Well, yeah, actually," I say. "But that's not it." I sit on the empty chair she has in her cubicle. Only a few workstations have a second chair. I was visiting her so much that Amber found one from an empty cubicle of a colleague who quit a few weeks ago.

"What's wrong?" she asks, confused.

"It's Kev," I say.

She purses her lips. "Oh, another fight? You said things were getting better."

"We didn't fight," I say. "Someone texted him this morning. They said they 'had a fun time last night'." As I say what was written, I examine Amber's face. I imagine if she doesn't respond as frantically as I did this morning that I spiralled out of control for no reason. Thankfully, that's not the case.

"What?" she says, confused. "Who sent that message to him?" Her face is full of expression, and I sense a slight bit of frustration as well, which makes me feel better.

"It wasn't a number saved on his phone," I say. "I don't even remember the number. I've been so out of it.

All I know it started with a four zero three, so it's local. I think there was an eight after that. I don't know. My mind is scrambled."

"So, what did Kev say?" she asks. I stare blankly at her. "Who did he say texted him?"

I take a deep breath. "I didn't ask him." Before she gives me crap over not asking, I tell her why. "Things have been rough lately. Last night, though, was great. He came back from the bar late, and when he went to bed, he woke me up in a wonderful way." I smile at her, and she lets out a laugh.

"You should have just asked him," she says.

I shake my head. "I don't want to come off like one of those crazy women who think that everything their husband does shows he's not faithful."

"But it's weird," she says. "That doesn't sound like another dude messaging him."

I nod. "I know. It's driving me crazy. I just wish I could figure out who it was."

She shakes her head and purses her lips. "When I thought my ex was cheating on me, I went a little crazy. The amount of gaslighting he did to me was unreal. Made me feel like I was actually going nuts. Meanwhile, he *was* cheating. I snooped on his phone trying to find out the truth, but he had changed his password."

"Kev changed his password too," I say, embarrassed. "I tried to unlock his phone after I saw the text but it's not the same." When I look at Amber, her eyes are wide. I turn my head and fight the urge to cry in front of her.

She catches on and taps the side of my leg. "Well, I'm sure Kev isn't cheating. Not like that jerk ex of mine. Kev's a good man."

She says that despite not even knowing him. Kev

never comes out to our bar nights after work. We used to go out regularly.

Amber only knows Kevin through my stories about him. Of course, she only knows the positives or big fights that happen.

"It just doesn't make sense," I say. "Who would text him a message like that so early in the morning?"

Amber purses her lips again, waiting a few moments to respond. "With my ex, I ended up getting his phone records."

"You can get someone else's phone records?" I say, confused.

She nods. "So long as you share a phone plan together you can. My ex and I did. We lived together for over a year. So, since we shared the same provider, we got a shared plan, and I found out I could get access to who called him." She smiles at me. "Well, turns out the woman from his work I knew was always hitting on him was more than just friends with him." She shakes his head. "Ugh, I still remember how pissed I was when I found her number on the list."

I look at her blankly. "What about text messages? Did you have access to that?"

She shakes her head. "Just calls in and out."

I could curse out loud but instead bit my lip and look away.

"There's no shame in getting the records," she says. "Do you share an account together?" I nod my head. "Well," she continues, "it's super easy to get them. Just walk into your provider's store and ask for them. They don't hassle you with questions or anything. You just tell them how many months you want the records for." She lets out a laugh. "I got six months' worth."

I take a deep breath. "I can't," I say. "I told you how I snooped on his phone a few months ago. Well, the guilt got to me so much that I told him about it. I'm sure that's why he changed his password."

She lets out another laugh. "Against my instructions, you told him," she reminds me. She was right. I shouldn't have come clean to Kev.

"Well, if I start getting phone records and snooping through what he's been doing, I'll feel worse. Like some weird detective trying to discover what's wrong with their life."

Amber shakes her head. "No shame in finding out the truth."

Moments ago, Amber said Kevin was a good man and wasn't the cheating type. Suddenly, she's encouraging me to snoop further. Before I can ask her why she changed her mind, Mr. Dunstrow, our boss, enters the cubicle.

"Morning, ladies," he says, fixing his bowtie. The fluorescent lights above shine on his receding hairline. "We're being a little loud this morning. I'd like you guys to speak a little lower please. I think you need to also return to your cubicle, Mrs. McNeil."

Amber smiles at him, and I reassure him that I'm leaving. He smiles back at Amber before leaving and patrolling the rest of the cubicles. He passes by the emergency exit door that leads to the parking lot outside. How I'd love to shove him out of the way and escape.

Amber rolls her eyes after he leaves and shakes her head. "Lunch today?" she asks.

"Maybe," I say.

I don't want to tell her how terrible I feel this morning. The last thing I need is more bad, greasy food for lunch.

"I'm sure it's not what you think," Amber says. "And if you're really worried, you can always get the phone records."

I let out a laugh. "Thanks, but I couldn't. I'd feel weird. I trust Kev."

CHAPTER 4

I flip through the pages of stapled phone records for the month of May. There's over ten pages. Kevin calls a lot more people than I thought. He is on his phone often, but I never see him calling anyone. When I ask him what he's doing on his phone, he always tells me he's just looking at online forums or messaging his work buddies. Doomscrolling the net.

Ugh. If only I could get records of his text messages, I could solve this mystery quickly. Instead, all I have are numbers. Random ten digits. None of the numbers tell me who they are. Life would be so much easier if they were each labelled "Mom" or "Sister". Instead, I have to cross reference my cell with the numbers on his records. I was able to quickly erase half the numbers, crossing out ones belonging to family members. I was surprised I had a few of his friends' numbers too. One was from a random message from his friend Adam when Kev's cell died while he was out and he wanted to let me know where he was.

Amber was right. It's extremely easy to get phone records for someone else's number when you share an account. I was so nervous walking into the store and asking for phone records of my husband's cell.

Amber was wrong on one part though. The man asked me why I wanted the records. I froze in place for a moment until he asked me if I was worried about being overcharged. I blurted out yes as the man stared at me awkwardly. I was so taken back that I stumbled further when he asked me what months I wanted records for. At first, I told him two months but slowly that turned to four, and then six.

I smiled awkwardly as the man printed out all the records for me, taking the time to staple each month as well.

I left the store determined to find the truth. After crossing out the numbers I knew, I was left with a dozen or so left. It took me a while to figure out what to do next. I need to know who these numbers belonged to. I can't exactly call them directly though. How awkward would it be if I called and hung up on them only for them to call back?

I'd have no solid reason to be calling them randomly. Telling the truth would almost certainly end worse.

Searching online, I remembered about star six nine calls. It's been over a decade since I used the phone number blocking number. Any time you call someone, if you dial star six nine before entering the number you want to call, you'll remain anonymous.

Ms. Q jumps on the couch, knocking the phone record out of my hand.

"Not now, Q," I say. But my cat doesn't understand I'm having a meltdown. If she could understand, she'd probably comment on how crazy I am for obtaining my husband's phone records, before licking her butt.

I start with a number Kevin called two days ago that I don't recognize. The same number is on the phone list several times in the past month as well.

As I dial the number, I frantically hang up before

calling, realizing I managed to forget to hit star six nine. My nerves are so shot that I can't function properly.

This time, I manage to block my number before calling. With each ring, my heart beats faster. Nobody picks up, though. I hang up, feeling even more defeated, my sense of self loathing getting worse.

I open a small bag of gummy worms I have on the living room table in front of me as I start to dial another number. This time I don't have to wait long before someone answers.

When I hear a man's voice, I cover my mouth, and the half-eaten gummy is trapped inside. I instantly know who it is. Kev's colleague James has an unusually raspy voice. I don't even breathe, fearing he'll know it's me. I quickly hang up, catching my breath and swallowing the remaining gummy.

I quickly looked at my phone, worried if I dialed star six nine before calling James's number. Thankfully, I did. I imagine what it would be like if he called me back on my cell, finding out that his friend's wife is calling him.

I have no clue what I would say in response.

"Sorry, just trying to figure out if my husband is having an affair. Well, see you around."

What am I doing? I look at the phone records and the remaining numbers to call. I cross off James's and let out a sigh.

Even though I feel stupid for doing it, it's as if my fingers have a mind of their own as they dial the next number. I clear my throat as I put my phone to my ear. My heart quickens as nobody picks up right away.

"What am I doing?" I say out loud.

I imagine how I must look. Phone records surround me on the couch as I try to sort out, organize and highlight numbers.

As I'm about to hang up, my eyes widen when a woman answers.

"Hello," she says with a cheerful voice.

I knew it. This is the woman. I'm not crazy for doing this. Part of me wants to yell at her, "Who the hell are you?"

But before I can let out a word, she tells me, "Thanks for calling Happy Smiles Dentistry. This is Beth. How can I make you smile today?"

My cell phone slips from my hand and hits the couch. I shake my head as I can hear the muffled voice of the woman asking if I'm still there. I slowly grab my cell and disconnect the call and Beth's happy-sounding voice.

How stupid am I? What am I doing?

I cross another number off the phone list and look at the remaining ones. Am I seriously going to keep going down the list? I'll give myself a heart attack at this rate, and for what? To find out my husband wants to book a cleaning with Beth?

I open my cell, but instead of dialing the next number, I text Amber. "I got the records and called several people. None of them were a surprise. I feel like a psycho." I hit send and look at my text to Amber, focusing on the word "psycho".

That's exactly what I am.

That must have been how I came off to Kev this morning. All the questions I asked him about where he was last night. What have I become? I look at the piles of records. Whatever I am now, I don't like it. I grab all the papers and put them into a pile.

No more dialing strangers tonight.

I look at my cell. Maybe Kevin and I can have a last-minute date night. I don't remember the last time we had an unplanned night out together. A random midweek date would help how I feel.

I open my phone and text Kev. "Hey, do you want to go out tonight? Dinner and a movie maybe?"

I smile when I text and to my surprise the message shows a little check mark at the bottom of the screen, meaning that Kev has read it. Little dots appear at the bottom. He's writing back to me. I hope he says yes. I'm craving his attention right now.

If only he knew what I was up to today, he'd certainly respond with a no. Who wants to go out with a clingy wife? A wife who goes so low as to get phone records to find out if their husband is cheating isn't a nice way to start a romantic evening.

Suddenly, the dots stop. I wait for his reply, but nothing happens. No more indication that he's writing back either. I feel crazy as I stare at my screen, waiting on tenterhooks for my husband to reply.

Realizing it won't happen soon, I open a browser on my cell. As if my brain won't let me rest, I start typing out a search. "How to tell if your husband's cheating."

The screen takes a moment to update with the search results. Instead of clicking on an article, the search engine's AI summarizes several points at the top. AI is taking over the internet completely now as well.

AI summarizes several answers, although I'm unsure where the source is from. "If your partner suddenly loses weight, has motivation for going to the gym or change of wardrobe, this may be an indication that there is someone new in their life. If they aren't making the changes for you, who are they making them for?"

At first, I rolled my eyes at the AI's assumption that this could be because of an affair. What if this person just wants to improve their life? After all, that's why Kevin did it.

I suddenly sigh with the realization that this point fits Kevin completely.

Kevin's lost around twenty pounds in the past few months. He's down to a trim hundred and sixty pounds. His lean muscles show easily in anything he wears. He's been hitting the gym several times a week. Just last week he came home with several bags of new clothes.

Part of me is jealous about how well he's been sticking to his diet and workouts. I could lose some weight and asked if I could come with him. He said he'd prefer if I do my own thing. I was hurt at first until he explained that the gym is where he goes to decompress. It's his time to get his head sorted out so he doesn't take his frustration home with him.

I can understand that.

Suddenly, an image of Stacy Wingham is beside him in my imagination, running on a treadmill as he's benching some heavy weights. My mind turns this into a nightmare with Stacy asking him to spot her with her set.

Kev tells me he gets a discount at a local gym because of his job. Did Stacy take advantage of the same discount?

I shake my head and close my phone. What does AI know about what's happening in my life? There's no way for a machine to tell if a partner is cheating or not.

I sigh again, staring at the pile of cell phone records in front of me.

What. Am. I. Doing?

My cell phone rings, and I pick it up immediately.

"Hey," I say, waiting to hear Kev's voice.

"Hey," Amber says back. "Are you okay?"

I sigh once again. "No. I've been calling random numbers, cross-referencing numbers from my own cell, and I feel absolutely embarrassed with myself. I feel so lost right now."

There's silence on the phone for a moment before Amber's cheerful voice continues. "Come out with us," she says. "It's been a while since you came to the bar with the gang. We're meeting up at the place across the street from our office at seven. Twenty-cent wings." She makes a clicking sound with her mouth, trying to entice me with cheap meat.

The thought of going to a bar makes me think of Kevin and what he did last night.

"I had fun last night. Let's do that again sometime." The text message has been haunting me all day.

Did he even go to the bar with his friends, or was that a cover? The whole thing makes me exhausted.

"Come on, Jo. Josie McNeil," she says with an authoritarian voice, "your presence is required at the bar immediately!"

Before I can turn her down, the front door opens. Kevin enters the living room. His expressionless face looks at me and the stack of papers on the table in front of me.

CHAPTER 5

"Hey," Kev says as he enters the living room. He immediately notices the pile of paperwork in front of me. "What are you doing?"

There's an awkward pause as I stare at the phone records and my husband's confused expression. He's home much earlier than expected.

"Uh, hey," I say, unable to hide my embarrassment. I'm surprised when my startled brain comes up with an excuse. "Work has some new policies and they want us to try looking them over. Hopefully, we'll have less requests for a supervisor callback." I smile and almost want to pat myself on the back for coming up with such a solid excuse in a moment.

Before he can figure out I'm lying, I lean over and grab the paperwork. There's an awkward moment when Q paws at my hand and stack of papers.

Not a time to play, Q. Please don't. I imagine her pawing the records to the floor, revealing my lies for Kev to see.

I manage to win the fight for the papers against my cat and shuffle them in my hands. "How was work?" I ask, trying to slide the paperwork to the side of my body, hugging it tightly.

Kev wasn't supposed to come home for another

hour. Usually, I'd be happy to see him, but I'd like to ask him to leave so I can properly hide my craziness.

"Good," he says, looking at me oddly.

"I figured it would be another late night for you with your deadline," I say, standing up in front of the couch. I need to get the phone records out of this room and away from his eyes before he realizes how insane his wife is.

"I wanted to come home early," he says with a thin smile. "Been working so much lately that I felt like a much-needed break." He takes out his cell. "You wanted to do dinner, right? I was going to text back, but I was already close to the house. What did you have in mind?"

I let out a nervous laugh. "Chinese? Sushi? Gyros? Whatever you feel like." I walk past him, holding the paperwork closer to my chest and covering it with both my hands. It would only take a quick glance to realize that I'm not telling the truth.

"Good," he says. "Chinese sounds perfect. Let's go to that place downtown. That place that created ginger beef. It tastes just like candy."

"Mmm," I say playfully. "Let me get ready really quick." I turn and attempt to leave the room when he calls out to me.

"Jo," he says with a tone. "What are you doing?" His voice almost sounds irritated, until I turn and see his playful smile.

"What?" I ask, confused, gripping the papers in my hand.

He tilts his head. "A kiss and or hug for your husband would be nice. He lets out a laugh. "You're acting so weird."

I let out a breath as I step towards him. He kisses me softly on the lips, and for a moment, my anxieties and worries melt away. All I want is to feel this moment.

As my body loosens to the warmth of his lips, my grip slips. One of the stapled months of phone records drops from my hands to the floor. In horror, I try to grab it, but Kev is faster.

He bends down and picks it up, examining it. "What did you say this was?"

"I, uh..." As I stumble over my words, Kevin figures it out for himself.

"This is my number," he says, pointing at the top of the report. "These are numbers I've called." He looks at the rest of the papers in my hand sternly. He quickly grabs another batch of records from me, tearing one of the stapled pieces in half. "My phone records," he says. "How many months do you have?" He looks at me with a mix of confusion and anger. "What the hell, Jo?"

"I can explain," I say, trying to find the words.

"Well!" Kev shouts, "I'm waiting. What possible reason could you have? Why would you have this? How? How can you get my phone records?"

I'm tempted to tell him what Amber at work told me. Somehow, I know that at this moment, telling him that since we share a plan, I'm entitled to get his records if I want, will not help this situation.

"Who did you have 'fun' with last night?" I ask, changing the subject to what really matters.

"What?"

"I saw the text from whoever texted you this morning. That's what she said to you. That she had fun last night."

"She?" Kev says with a tone. "What the hell are you talking about?"

I sigh. "I know you saw the text message. I saw

it before you woke up. You changed your password so I couldn't see who it was." I think of the AI summarized search I did. "What are you hiding?"

Kev takes a step back from me, tossing the phone records in his hands to the floor. "You actually think I'm, what? Cheating on you?" He shakes his head and looks up at me slowly. "We made love last night. I had fun with *you*. At least, I thought the feeling was mutual."

I step towards him, but he backs away. "Yes," I say, pleading with him to understand. "I had so much fun with you last night. I just need—"

Kev puts up a hand in a gesture for me to be quiet. "That's enough, Josie. Honestly. It's been rough lately for us. Maybe you felt the tension. Maybe not. Most days I try to ignore what's happening in this marriage. But last night I felt things were getting better. Instead, today you start accusing me of cheating on you." He shakes his head again. "I don't know what to do with you."

"Kev!" I say, softening my voice. "I'm just confused. I want us to be better too. I saw that text, though, and I got scared. I don't want to lose you. I love you."

He scoffs. "You love me? You think I'm cheating and come at me like this. You invade my privacy in the—" He looks at the papers on the floor. "—weirdest way possible." He picks up one of the sheets and sees my scribbled names beside numbers and pen markings crossing them off. "This is scary, Jo." He looks at me with fire in his eyes. "Who are you?"

I put up my hands in surrender. "Sorry, Kev. I'm not trying to act this way. I just freaked out."

"I know," he scoffs again.

"Let's take a break from this conversation," I say. "Maybe we can come back and talk about it when we've cooled off."

He looks outside the window. "I'm going to go out." His voice is calmer now. I hate when our fights escalate quickly into shouting matches. I find that taking a break helps us both speak calmer and more respectfully to each other.

"Okay," I say. "That works. I was going to go out with some work people too."

He shakes his head. "Who are you going out with?"

I nod and take a deep breath. "Some of the usual gang from work. Amber invited me. Trey will be there. And—"

"Trey," Kev says with a smirk and tilts his head. "Your little board game buddy? Your ex?"

"Ex?" I say, surprised. Kev knows we never actually dated. "It was one date, Kevin. We kissed once."

He lets out a laugh. "I see what you're doing. You're acting crazy like this. I've seen it before, Jo. I know. This is all projection. Mary acted the same way. And then I found out what she was really up to. She was the one cheating. Is that what you're doing here?"

I'm shocked and I'm sure my face shows it. "Kev, I would never."

"I should get your phone records. I should make you unlock your phone and see all your messages, emails, everything." When I don't respond, he nods. "You don't like how this feels, do you? Imagine how I feel."

"Kev, I'm sor—"

"Sorry?" he says, beating me to it. "First, you snoop on my phone. Now, you somehow get my phone records. What's next, Jo? Are you going to start following me everywhere I go?"

"I'm not like that," I try to explain myself, but Kev

shakes his head at me and opens the front door. "Where are you going?" I ask.

"Out!" he shouts, slamming the door behind him.

CHAPTER 6

"I'm such a psycho," I say out loud, covering my eyes.

"No, you're not." Trey sips his beer and looks at Amber.

"You had every right to have questions," she says. She puts her hand on mine and squeezes. "I would have a lot of questions if my boyfriend had messages like that on his phone."

We sit at the end of a long table. It's been a while since I've come to the bar after work. A lot more people are here. Thankfully, most of them seem more interested in whatever they're talking about.

I shake my head and slump in the bar chair. "Why the hell did I actually get phone records?" I look at Amber. "I wish you'd never told me about it. I found absolutely nothing out."

"Nothing?" Trey asks.

"Nada! I know he's spoken to his dentist," I say with a laugh. "Ugh. What was I thinking? Imagine finding your wife searching through actual phone records. He must think I'm a lunatic. Some psycho wife."

Amber lets out a sigh. "Well, next time, you have to do it more sneakily. You don't search the records in a place where he can find you looking at them."

I scoff. "Amber, I'm not a pro at this like you."

"Sorry," she says with a small smile. "But I mean, I was just telling you about what happened with my ex. These days, cheaters have a whole different system to keep what they do secret. They use WhatsApp or have second phones."

"Second phones?"

"Like a burner phone?" Trey asks. The question gets the attention of another coworker, who looks at us, confused, before she continues drinking her martini and goes back to her conversation with other coworkers near her.

"Sort of," Amber says. "A phone to keep all their secrets more... secret."

"Well, if he had a second phone, I think I'd have seen it by now," I say.

"They hide it well. That's why they have a second phone to begin with. They want to keep it all secret."

Trey shakes his head with a smirk. "Amber, how do you know all these cheating tips and tricks?"

She lets out a laugh. "Let's just say my dating life's been complicated." She looks at me and her smile vanishes. I'm sure my expression shows nothing except confusion and sadness at the moment. "It's going to be okay, Josie. Like you said, you didn't find anything on his phone records."

"What did he tell you about the text message?" Trey asks. Amber looks at me, taking a sip of her cocktail mix.

I let out a deep breath. "Well, he didn't say. He just got upset when he saw the phone records. Really upset, actually. He stormed out."

Amber stirs her small straw in her glass. "He didn't even explain who sent the text?"

"He didn't tell me who it was," I say again. I glance

down at the dirty bar floor. When I look up, both Trey and Amber look at me strangely. "Stop," I say to them. "I can't keep doing this."

"Doing what?" Trey asks.

"It's driving me crazy," I say. "I need to trust him. Kev wouldn't do something like this. In the time I've known him, he's never lied to me."

"Well," Trey says, taking another sip of his beer, "no lie that you caught him in."

I look at him in anger. Why is he trying to get me to second-guess my husband's intentions? Maybe Kevin was right to be upset that I'm going out to a bar with Trey. Instead of responding, I shake my head and stand up.

"I'm going to go back home," I say. "Hopefully, Kev will be back soon." I look at my cell quickly. Kevin hasn't responded. I've sent several texts and calls, but he hasn't responded to any. The green check below my texts show that he's read them though.

"We're just worried about you," Amber says.

We? How much have they talked about me before I came to the bar? I look at the rest of the table of coworkers. Were they all talking about me behind my back?

All this talk about phone records, second phones and apps has my head spinning.

"I have to trust him," I say. "He's my husband. If I can't believe what he says, why stay married?"

"Jo," Amber says empathetically. "We're here for you, okay?"

Trey nods. "We're just looking out for you."

I feel like the longer I talk to my friends, the crazier I become. "I'll see you guys tomorrow," I say, gathering my purse and jacket before leaving the table.

CHAPTER 7

I toss and turn in bed. It's nearly eleven at night and Kev hasn't returned. He hasn't called or texted. Nothing.

I have no clue where my husband is and it's making me super anxious. Why won't he respond to me? How angry is he? Has he calmed down since our conversation or has the time away from me made him somehow angrier?

"Maybe this time he'll leave you," the nasty voice inside me says. "Maybe he's with someone. A woman."

I put a pillow over my head to stop the voices inside me from making my anxiety worse. Where's Kev? Is he staying at a hotel instead of coming home? He's never done that after a fight.

It's something I've always taken pride in in our relationship. We always make up the same night we argue. Sure, sometimes when we fight, which isn't as often as I make it seem, it can take hours for us to calm down and talk normally to each other.

Typically, we'll start our making up process with a long hug, followed by both of us apologizing for how we acted. Then we talk out whatever started the issue and kiss. Water under the bridge after that.

What if he's had enough, though? I like to think we don't fight often, but what if Kevin feels differently?

What if there's too much water under our marriage bridge for him to shrug it off? The water's pouring over the bridge to the point where he can't ignore the issues we're having.

I told him before I was open to therapy. Of course, he has to be difficult.

A bright light shines into the bedroom window. Outside, I hear a car pull up. He's home, finally.

Only, I don't hear the garage door open. Our bedroom is directly above the two-car garage. Usually, I can hear the door open and close.

I stand up from the bed and look outside. A car I don't recognise is in our driveway. However, I know the driver.

Stacy Wingham.

Beside her, in the passenger seat, is Kevin. The two are talking to each other inside. Both are smiling wide. Kev nods to her and opens the passenger side door. Before he steps out, he touches her shoulder and waves at her. When he shuts the door, he turns to our house, and I duck, worried that he may have seen me watching.

He didn't. I peer outside again and now Kev's out of sight. For a moment, I'm thankful until I realize I was spotted.

Stacy is staring directly at me. There's an awkward pause. She doesn't wave or smile. Our eyes meet before she begins pulling out of the driveway.

Downstairs, I hear Kevin inside our house. I slide back into bed and try my best to pretend I'm resting. It feels like it takes hours for Kev to come into our bedroom.

When he does, I don't turn to him. Instead, I continue with my restful performance.

When he slides into the bedsheets, I immediately

smell the liquor on his breath. I don't have to ask him where he's been. I also don't have to ask him who he was with. Stacy Wingham was with him. I wonder who else, or if there was anyone else. His pretty little work wife went out with him after his real wife and him were in a fight.

I think about how my time with my friends went. The entire time, I talked about Kev and me. I remind myself of Amber's knowledge of infidelity.

What did Kevin say about me when he was out? I can only imagine.

"Hey guys, guess what my psycho wife did today?" he'd tell them. I can only imagine the shock on their faces as he explained walking into our house and seeing me review his phone records. I can see how happy that would make that stupid pretty face of Stacy's look. She'd be delighted to know she's one step closer to making her work husband her real one.

I try to calm myself as Kev settles down. Don't go to sleep angry. I need to resolve our fight before we go to bed. If we don't, I'll continue to toss and turn until morning.

I turn to him slowly. "Hey," I say.

He takes a moment to respond as he stares deeply into my eyes. "Hi."

"Did you have fun?" I ask.

He purses his lips. He's probably waiting for me to ask him a bunch of questions again like this morning. I won't do that, though. I'll show him he's married to a well-adjusted woman. I already threw away the phone records. I'll never do that again. I'll show my husband how much I trust him. He'll know how much I love him.

I won't even bring up Stacy, as hard as that is. I have so many questions. Why did she drive you home? Why not one of your guy friends? Why did it have to be her?

"Did you leave your car at the bar?" I ask.

He nods. "I had a little too much to drink," he says with a thin smile.

"I can drive you in the morning," I say.

So far, so good. Inside, my brain and voices are yelling in unison to demand answers. I won't listen to the background noise in my head. I need to start trusting my husband.

"Thanks," he says. He turns away from me and stares at the wall.

I place my hand on his back and massage it, not very well. "I'm sorry, Kev. Are you still angry?"

"I don't know what I am right now," he says calmly.

Well, I suppose that's better than him yelling at me.

"I'm sorry," I say again softly.

"It's just odd. I mean, how did you even get my phone records?"

I take a deep breath. "I found out you can get another person's records if you share the same plan."

"Josie, how did you even figure that out?" He turns to me, and our eyes meet. I'm waiting for him to look angry again, but he's not. Instead, he seems hurt.

"I'm sorry," I say again, hating how he looks at me. It's as if I took an emotional dagger and stabbed him through the heart. "Amber at work told me she caught an ex-boyfriend cheating that way. I—"

He shakes his head. "I would never do that to you. You know that, right? I just don't understand how you think I could."

"I'm sorry," I say again.

He purses his lips, raising his hand from underneath the sheets and placing it softly on the side of my face, caressing me. "Is this about her?" he asks.

With how he's asking, I know who he's referring to without him saying it. "I don't know," I say.

"After we lost her, I said you should do therapy," he says.

I nod on the pillow. "I know you did. I wanted you to come with me, though."

He takes another deep breath. "I'm fine, Jo. I think you need to talk to someone. This is starting to impact us."

"Well, let's do it together, then."

He stares at me as he caresses my face more. "It's not your fault. What happened isn't because of anything you did, do you hear me?"

I stare at his soft blue eyes, letting his loving gaze put me at ease. "I know."

"Good," he says. "Everything's going to be okay. Someday, when you're ready, we can try again."

My mouth purses as he says the words. I try my best to hide the pain.

What if I don't want to try again?

CHAPTER 8

Trey looks at his playing cards, attempting his best to count his points. No matter how many times we play, it always amazes me how terrible he is at math.

"Fifteen-one," he says, counting an eight and a seven. "Ah." He looks at his nine and six. "Fifteen-two."

I smile, as I tell him I have ten points, quickly. When I move my peg ten slots, I'm happy with the progress. A couple more winning hands and I'll easily skunk him. Skunking someone in a crib is when you win by a large number of points. It's the ultimate defeat that crushes your soul when it happens to you.

It doesn't happen often, though. Trey and I have a running bet. Whoever gets skunked has to buy the other coffee. There's a gourmet coffee place a few blocks away from our office.

"Mocha with extra whipped cream," I say with a smile.

"It's not over," he says playfully. "I won't win, but I won't get skunked." I let out a laugh as I shuffle the cards for the next round. As I do, Trey smirks. "You had 4 diamonds in your hand and forgot to count them."

I sigh as I realize he's right. He's not the best at math but apparently can tell the difference between suited cards better than me, at least today.

"You're lucky we're not playing muggins," he says with a laugh. Muggins is where you can steal other players' points if they miscount their score for the round.

I don't tell him that my mind is elsewhere. Playing crib with Trey is a welcomed distraction instead of sitting in my cubicle trying not to think about my conversation with Kev.

We didn't go to bed angry at least. We seemed to have made up before sleeping and that's what's most important. Still, I'm worried, if I could read my husband's mind, how scary his thoughts would be.

My actions were intense. I jumped straight away to an extreme. I meant what I said to Kevin when I apologized. I know I must have come off like a crazy woman.

Amber walks into Trey's cubicle. "Hey guys," she says, looking at the board. "Oh, someone's about to get skanked."

"Not skanked," Trey says.

"Skunked," I confirm.

She lets out a laugh. "You two are like an old couple, I swear." She looks at me. "Are you okay?"

I sit back in the chair. "When Kev came back home last night, we talked for a little bit. He's not angry at me, not exactly, I guess. He seems more concerned about me. My mental health or whatever."

Amber and Trey glance at each other and back at me.

"What you've been through is a lot, Jo," Amber says. "To lose a pregnancy in your second tri—I mean, it's unexpected."

"I know," I say. "Kev even talked about trying again."

"Really?" Trey says, surprised.

"I'm not ready though. I don't think I ever will be."

Amber rests her hand behind my neck. "It's okay to take as long as you need."

I realize I'm being a little loud. I hate cubicles. Sometimes you genuinely believe nobody else can hear you with the fake walls that surround you.

"Did he tell you who messaged him?" Trey says. I'm surprised he's bringing it up. "You guys made up, but did he tell you who messaged him with that text?"

I shake my head. "I didn't bring it up again. I'm done. I meant what I said that I needed to trust him. I'll make myself go crazy if I continue like this."

Amber nods. "That's probably for the best."

Maybe they're worried for me, but they don't know the full extent of when I went the first time I snooped on Kev's phone. I pulled up his Facebook and tried looking at his activity on the app. Kevin has never so much as posted a selfie in his entire life on his profile. He never uses it except to keep in contact with friends from across the country that he doesn't see much anymore.

I hate it when I spiral like this. I'm letting all my insecurities run my emotions. That always leads to overeating or making poor decisions. Today will be different. I even made a salad for lunch.

I start dealing out cards and look at Amber. "Our anniversary is coming up," I say. Trey and I play our cards and move our pegs on the board.

"What are you guys going to do?" she asks.

"I'm not sure." I move my peg four points after a solid play. Trey shakes his head in dismay as I get closer to winning the entire game with him behind the skunk line.

"What did you guys do your first anniversary?" Amber asks.

"They went to that cabin, right?" Trey says as he attempts to count his points.

I'm surprised he remembers. "That's right," I say. "It's a few hours' drive, but the cabin is right on the lake. Very secluded."

Trey laughs. "Don't forget to mention how you're afraid to be there because of the bears." He looks at Amber.

"Bears?" Amber repeats. "Yeah, I don't think so. Take me to a motel instead."

I shake my head at Trey. "It's not that bad there. Kev loves it. He's been there a few times in the past. He's gone hunting there before. I like it there."

Trey shakes his head after I say the words, but I'm not sure if it's because I'm about to win or what I said. I manage to smile as I show my cards. I have twelve points. Trey double counts it as I place my peg at the end of the board and win the game. I gleefully point at his peg. "Skunked. So, grande, mocha, extra whipped cream."

Trey laughs. "No mercy, I tell you. Lucky is all you are."

I don't know how lucky I feel though.

"You skunked me even without counting your points correctly." He shakes his head again. "So lucky we said no muggins."

"*Muggins*?" Amber laughs. "This game is so lame. I feel fifty years older hearing you say the word 'muggins' out loud."

I laugh. To my surprise Trey doesn't. Instead, he stares at me, removing his peg from the board.

CHAPTER 9

I sit on the couch, flicking through the stations aimlessly. Nothing seems to be interesting enough to watch. I've already gone through lists of movies and shows on Prime and Netflix, but again nothing caught my attention.

I look at the time and realize Kev should be home soon.

It's been a week since we had our blowout. Things are better, but not exactly fine. We talked and I feel like we made up but not in our usual fashion. Typically, we'd make love soon after a big blowout in a way to mend fences. The only part about having a blowout that I enjoy is the sex afterwards. Usually, it's much more intense. It's as if we're trying to show each other how much we care for one another with our bodies.

Our bedroom has just been for sleeping lately, though. I'm not sure why. When I brought it up to Kevin, he told me things at work have been stressful. With him being over his deadline, I'm sure it is. He was supposed to conclude his research a few weeks ago. Now he and his team are out a large bonus, and the pressure is still on.

I asked what happened again. He explained it to me, but I have no understanding what he does in his world as a principal research scientist. His work has something to do with data and chemical compounds. Apparently, Health Canada is breathing down his team's neck.

He's been coming home late a lot lately. Thankfully, my own anxiety about the reasons why haven't been so strong. I meant what I told myself last week. I need to trust my husband.

I never brought up my concerns about why Stacey Wingham drove him home last week. I don't ask him questions about who he's going out with after work at the bar. The last few nights, he's been coming home after ten at night. Obviously, he's not working in the office the entire time.

Can I blame Kev for wanting to let off steam? Even if that steam is with a woman like Stacy.

I know why I get jealous of her too. That's the frustrating part of this. Stacy is gorgeous. Kev is amazingly handsome.

Me? Well, I don't like how I look or feel about myself these days.

I know I let myself go. I know some of the reasons why I let myself go. After we lost her, it's been so difficult. I feel like some people would tell me to just get over it.

It's not that easy.

All I have left of her is the high blood sugar level I had while carrying her. I just need to eat healthier. Lose some weight. Be more active.

I have the best husband to motivate me to be more active.

I sigh as I sit around the living room watching television. Or at least attempting to. I should be going out for a run or something. Amber mentioned wanting to do yoga together. I could take her up on the offer.

It would be frustrating to find out the lack of

flexibility I have, though. Plus, Amber knows how to yoga. I'd look stupid attempting it. I wish you could fast forward the awkward part of getting more active to a time where you look confident in what you're doing.

I stop on a channel and lower the remote when I see the headline. "Missing Calgary Woman Found Dead".

I raise the volume and listen to the newsman. "The body of Jodi Lawson, who's been missing for over two weeks, has been discovered by hikers in Kananaskis County. Authorities have confirmed that her body was found off-trail by a pair of hikers late yesterday evening. They also confirm that foul play is still being investigated. Police are asking for anybody with any information on this case to come forward. Jodi Lawson was last seen—"

I shake my head in disbelief. Such a tragedy. A young woman with so many years ahead of her. I remember hearing about her going missing. Automatically, people tend to think the worst. Of course she's dead. But when it's confirmed, it's devastating in a whole new way.

Taking a deep breath, I pick up the remote to change the channel. Instead, I'm mesmerized by the picture of the young woman on the screen.

Here I am complaining about my problems when this woman's life has come to an end. All the issues she had going on prior to her death will forever be left unresolved. It really makes you think about what matters in life.

I've been so stressed out over that text message that Kev received that I could barely function the day I read it. Again, I know why I'm this way. It all boils down to my own insecurities. I'm not happy in my own skin.

That's why I'm trying to do better. I threw away the chips and candy at work today. I emptied the pantry at home of anything terrible. Whenever I have urges for something sweet, I eat a large bowl of salad and wait fifteen minutes. If I'm still craving something bad, I have some low-calorie fudge popsicles that don't have many carbs or sugar in them.

I have a system. I'm happy with myself for even coming up with something. It feels like I'm already on a better path.

That dumb voice inside me says that I'll go back to my old ways as soon as I get stressed. If I mess up once, I'll try and give myself some grace and get back on track.

I look at the screen, at the young woman who was found dead in the woods. I hope they find out what happened to her.

A knock on the door breaks my thoughts. I stand up from the couch, disrupting Q's slumber on my lap. As I slowly stand up, the news shows another picture of Jodi with some family members. She looks barely over twenty. The picture of her with who I assume are her parents is from what looks like a university graduation ceremony.

I open the front door, surprised.

Nobody's there. I didn't take that long to get off the couch. I take a step outside and look around the empty porch. I turn my head both ways, looking at the sidewalks. On one side, I see a red car noisily driving away. Going the opposite way, a woman in dark workout attire is jogging down the block, her blond ponytail bouncing with each step.

Confused, I step back into my house, nearly slipping on something beneath my feet. I'm even more confused seeing the red cardboard under my foot. It's in the shape of a heart. I can see it's some kind of a letter that's too perfectly placed to be random.

Frightened, I step away from it. What's more unsettling isn't the odd letter itself but the words on it. Each letter on the front is cut out from newspaper clippings, forming words.

I bend over and pick it up, reading it again, my eyes widening with confusion and fear.

"Read me now."

CHAPTER 10

With the heart-shaped letter in my hand, I let my arm drop, looking around outside again for who could have left this at my door.

The young woman is getting further away down the block, her bobbing ponytail barely visible now. Other cars are driving down my street. I try to peer into the windows of the vehicles. One of them smiles at me and waves.

Sara Mckenzie. She lives a few houses down from me. She and I are pretty friendly with each other, but not today. Her face sours when I don't wave back.

How can I? I'm paralyzed with the letter in my hand. Something about the cutout letters makes it even more frightening. I've seen movies where bad guys leave terrible notes like this. It's always some kind of ransom letter.

Slowly, I open the letter to read what's inside.

"Call this number," it says in jaggedly glued newspaper letters. My mouth opens as I read the digits listed below. Scared, I read the rest of the message below it. "Do not tell him or anybody else about this letter. OR ELSE."

I read the message over again, not understanding why someone would leave such a scary letter outside my door.

Part of me wants to call the police immediately. I read the last part of the message again, warning me not to do so. Whoever sent the message made sure to warn me about telling anyone with capital letters.

Who would leave this at my door? Why?

Scared, I glance around again, looking everywhere. There are cars parked along the sidewalk. What if whoever sent the message is still here?

That would make sense. Besides the woman jogging, I didn't see anybody else around my house. Whoever sent it could have been hiding in their car.

I could investigate this right now. I could find out if someone is lurking outside my house, watching me from their vehicle as I read their frightening message.

The clipped-out letters are designed to scare me, I know it. And it's working. I quickly go inside, shutting the front door hard and locking it. In my state of fear, I realize I had gone into the backyard and watered some tomato plants an hour ago. Did I lock the back door? I run past my living room as Q watches me. In the kitchen, I check and thankfully it's locked. I look outside the small window in the back door, worried about what I'll see.

Nobody's there. Down on the wooden steps, there's nothing out of the ordinary except the watering can I left near my plants.

I look at the front of the red cardboard letter. It's handmade. Someone took the time to make it for me.

"Read me. Now."

There's something authoritative about the message on the front. Whoever it is wants me to call the number. Not just wants but demands I do.

Why? Who will pick up if I call?

What if this is a ransom letter? When I call the

number, a voice will answer I don't recognize. They'll demand money or whatever.

In exchange for what? Kevin? If they want money, they chose the wrong couple. We have very little after buying this house a year ago.

I run into the living room and pick up my cell phone. I don't call the number the newspaper clippings demand I dial. Instead, I call Kev.

I need to know he's okay.

As I wait for him to pick up, I open the heart-shaped letter. "Do not call Kevin or anyone else."

Kev doesn't pick up; it goes to his voicemail. I hang up and don't leave a message.

I look at the number inside the letter. What happens if I don't do what this person wants? Why are they wanting me to call this number? What will happen if I tell Kevin?

I look at the television. The newsman continues talking about Jodi Lawson. "Local Woman's Body Found. Foul Play Suspected." Scared, I turn off the television.

Without the sound of the TV, the silence in the living room settles heavily around me. All there is me, and the heart-shaped letter trembling in my hand.

There's also the number inside. I open the letter and read it again. Curiosity is getting to me now.

I take my cell and slowly dial the number, taking a deep breath. Worried what will happen, I end the call but redial the number, only this time using star six nine. I hesitate before I hit the button to connect.

This is exactly what they want.

I hit the green button on my cell anyways. It's as if my finger has a mind of its own. I need to find out what's happening. Kev didn't pick up. A strange letter at my door told me to call this number.

I need to know what happens when I call it.

My cell continues to connect with whoever owns the number. I wait, worried who will pick up. What will they say when they do?

What will I say to them?

Who are you? That seems like an obvious way to start this conversation.

My heart flutters with each ring. After the sixth, with no one picking up, dread starts to creep in. What am I supposed to do now?

The letter didn't exactly say what to do. I'm supposed to just call this number. Isn't something supposed to happen?

Whose number is this even? Soon, a voicemail may start, and I'll find out. I don't plan on leaving a message of course, but I need to know who this number belongs to.

After the tenth ring I realize that it won't be that easy.

Suddenly, it hits me. The first number I called on the phone records didn't have a voicemail either. Am I calling the same number?

I hang up, giving up on the number listed in the anonymous letter.

I let out a sigh of frustration when I realize I threw away the phone records. I told myself I was done playing investigator. I wasn't going to keep going down the unknown numbers on my husband's list.

I smile when I remember that I called the number on my cell and I should be able to easily find it. I scroll through my call history on my cell until I start seeing the star six-nine numbers I called. When I see the first number I called, I look at the heart-shaped letter in my hand and compare the two.

They don't match.

Of course it's not that easy.

I look at the mysterious number in the letter and the one on my cell. What're the chances they're connected? I dial the number from Kev's phone record list again, hoping someone will pick up. I ensure I hit star six nine again before calling it. The last thing I need is for one of Kev's friends to pick up again and ask me why I'm calling them.

That's when I hear a car outside. I look out the front window and see Kev driving into the garage.

The number continues to ring, and nobody picks up. I see Kev leave the garage and head towards the front door. My eyes widen as I realize I'm still holding the heart-shaped letter in my hand.

"Do not tell him or anybody else about this letter. OR ELSE," the letter warned.

CHAPTER 11

When Kevin enters our house, he genuinely smiles at me. His endearing sense of being happy to see me makes me feel more guilty.

"Tell him," a voice says inside me.

I managed to hide the anonymous letter under the living room couch cushion before he came inside. When I don't greet him quickly, I worry he'll catch on that something's wrong. Last week, Kev knew instantly something was off with my expression and the stack of phone records in front of me. This time it's not as obvious.

I greet him with a hug and a peck on the lips. Q rubs her back between our legs.

"Tell him," the voice urges me.

I don't listen. My inner voice says a lot of terrible things. Why should I listen now?

"How was work?" I ask him.

Kevin sighs. "It was something. We got a lot done today, so for a change, no late night. I figured I'd come home." He lets out a laugh. "I know it's been hard lately. Thanks for understanding."

"I know you're going through a lot," I say. I glance at the couch, knowing what it's hiding. Q jumps on the cushion and my eyes widen. It's as if she knows what's underneath and wants to paw at it. I wonder what Kev would say if I showed him. Would he know the number? Is it a number saved on his phone?

Does it belong to the person who texted him last week?

So many questions. I feel my head spiraling, and I can't think straight. Why would someone leave such a frightening letter outside my house? Whose number is it?

It has to involve Kev. Why else would the letter demand I don't tell him about its existence?

Does that mean Kev is hiding something? I know how he reacted last time I came clean. Do I really want to go through that again?

A part of me is telling me to ignore the letter. Pretend it doesn't exist, but don't play along. Don't play the game it wants you to start.

"Pizza and a movie in?" Kev asks with a smile.

"Perfect," I say, managing a smile of my own. I'm barely able to keep it together, though. I want to tell my husband what happened. I'm nervous. The clipped newspaper letters are scary. Someone went out of their way to do this to me.

Why?

"Can you order?" Kevin asks, walking past me towards the stairs. "I'm going to take a nice long shower and try to get work off my brain."

Perfect, I think. I nod and tell him I'll get the usual order. The usual consists of a Mediterranean vegetable pizza with chicken.

He walks up the stairs slowly as I put the cell to my ear. I don't call the pizza place to order the usual though.

I can't stop myself. I need to know why someone left a letter outside my door with what feels like a random number inside.

I redial the number, ensuring I dial star-six nine again before I do. I wonder how much star six nine even costs. I've already used it a handful of times. I imagine if Kevin obtained my phone records he'd have a lot of questions.

The number rings as I wait impatiently for someone to pick up. I need someone to give me answers. Why would a letter give me a number where nothing happens?

Then again, nothing happens the second time I call. The number continues to ring. No voicemail appears to be attached.

How very anticlimactic.

I hear the shower turn on, and even from the basement, I can hear Kev humming some song. This time it's one I've heard before. "I Heard it Through the Grapevine". I wonder why he has such an old song on his mind.

"Don't play this game," the voice inside me says.

And yet I look at my cell, wanting to redial. None of it makes any sense. How can I rest not knowing why someone would do this to me?

Someone anonymous left a letter outside my house. Rang the doorbell and quickly escaped before I could see who they were.

There are teenagers on the block. I don't know the parents very well, but when they left on a short trip to Europe, their two teenaged sons took the opportunity to throw a mega party. Many of the neighbors were quite upset with the shenanigans of drunken underaged teens puking on their front yard.

What's the chance the letter is more shenanigans from these teens?

The letter isn't addressed to me specifically. It

doesn't mention my name or Kevin's. It's very generic. Call this number, or else.

There's something juvenile about someone knocking on my door and running away only for me to find a spooky letter.

I smile, thinking how stupid I am for getting so nervous over it. It's a prank. A joke. Kids having fun by scaring someone with a letter.

I slowly climb the steps and make my way into our bedroom. Kev's in the middle of the chorus of the Motown song in the shower.

At some point when he's done with his terrible shower karaoke and he comes to the bedroom, I'll tell him what happened. I'll show him the letter. The threat on the card is empty, especially if it's who I think it's from.

I take out some comfy clothes from the dresser and lay them on the bed. I change out of my work clothes for the cozy loose ones, my cell phone staring back at me as I do.

Inside, I'm battling the urge to call the number again. If it's a prank, it's a real dumb one. Why give me a number that nobody picks up? If it's a prank, shouldn't it be funny?

Another thought hits me. The teenagers that threw that party came off like the stereotypical lazy, sleeps-in-till-noon types. I don't suspect they would take the time to cut out letters and make a letter like the heart-shaped one hidden under the couch cushion.

Seems like a lot of work for very minimal laughs.

If it's a prank, wouldn't it be a number they could know what's happening on? Wouldn't they answer the phone and laugh uncontrollably at how frantic I am?

I pick up my cell, angry and scared all at once. I

dial the number with star six nine again, knowing that I'll likely get the same outcome as before. Nobody will answer. Just as before, nobody does.

In my anger, I don't immediately hear the sound coming from inside the bedroom. As the number rings again, I hear it better. Something is vibrating near me.

I look around the room, frantically trying to find the source. With another ring, I know the sound is closer to Kev's side of the bed. It's almost as if it's coming from under the bed. When I get to the edge of the nightstand, I hear it much clearer.

The nightstand has two drawers. I open the top one first but it's nearly empty. When I open the bottom, I see a blue light between Kev's underwear. I sift through the drawer and pick it up with a loose finger, my stomach tightening the moment I recognize what it is.

As Kev starts to whistle his song from inside the shower, I look at the bathroom door, unable to understand why he has this hidden in his drawer.

Kevin has a second cell phone.

CHAPTER 12

Kev grabs a slice of pizza, with half the toppings getting stuck to the rest of it. He makes a face and tugs at the missing toppings until they break free. With contempt, he tosses it in his mouth and takes a large bite of the top of the pizza crust.

I always found it weird how Kev eats his pizza. It's just weird eating a slice crust-first.

You know what else is odd? Him having a second cell phone.

I can hear Amber telling me a story about her cheating ex.

Now, here I am unable to think straight. An anonymous letter was left outside my house with a number inside. That number belongs to Kevin! He owns a second phone. A cell I had no clue existed.

Why?

I feel my blood pressure rising just thinking about it all.

Kev laughs at something happening on *Love is Blind*, the reality show we're watching. His laughter temporarily wakes Ms. Q, who's resting beside me. Instead of a movie, Kev wanted to continue with our show we've been marathoning. Although, with his work schedule, it's been hard to get into this season.

I enjoy watching any reality television show. There's something so fascinating about the drama and lives of these characters, even if it's likely scripted.

In *Love is Blind*, single strangers are put in opposite rooms where they can meet potential partners through a wall, but they can't see each other. Eventually, some of these strangers propose to each other. Only after proposing do they get to meet each other. I mean, who can get engaged to someone without seeing who they really are? Most of the marriages on the show don't end up working out, for obvious reasons. The main factor being they don't actually know each other. But some do.

The thought of it makes me question myself and my marriage.

How much do I know about Kev?

We married within a year of meeting. I fell head over heels for him instantly. He was so charming, handsome and funny. He has a way about him that when he talks to you, you feel like you're the only woman he's ever had eyes for.

I'd never felt so seen before by another man. Most of the boyfriends I had were nowhere as exciting as Kevin. Most men I've been with would entertain me for a little while, just enough to let me talk briefly before cutting me off so they could take over the conversation.

Not Kevin. He listened. I felt special. I liked how he made me feel. I can still remember the night he asked me to marry him.

But then, reality hits. The dreams I had for a family with him were ruined. The man I was head over heels for I feel wants nothing to do with me now. He's never home these days.

And now there's the letter. The letter confirms

something I never thought possible.

Kevin's cheating on me. It's just like Amber said. He uses a second cell to call his girls on the side.

Kevin takes another large bite of his pizza crust and wraps his arm around me. My entire body stiffens with his touch. He notices.

"You okay?" he asks. "Feels like you're shivering."

I take a small bite of the pizza I've been holding for minutes without tasting. "Good. Just watching the show," I say without looking at him. I don't want him to see my face. If he does, I'll break down and either shout or cry at him. It's hard to tell which reaction I'll have.

I need answers, though. Why does he have a second phone? Who is he cheating on me with? Then there's the text message he got last week from someone. The person he had a "fun" time with.

But if he has a second phone, why would this mystery woman message him on his main one? If he's cheating, why wouldn't he be better at it than this?

Cheaters always get caught. They mess up. If he's been going out with dates, there would be a trail. We not only share a cell plan but have a joint credit card. I could look through to see what inconsistencies there are.

I think of Amber. She's the one who explained to me how these cheaters operate. Some have second phones, which I now confirmed Kev has. How likely is it that he has a separate credit card in his name?

The thought of it makes me want to scream. The idea that we're sitting on this couch makes me uneasy, knowing what's beneath the cushion.

Nothing makes sense in my life anymore.

How easy would it be for me to show Kev the letter? I'd stand up, turn off the show, reveal the letter under the cushion and demand answers. As he comes up with some dumb excuse, I'd show him the second phone he's been hiding.

I'd watch him squirm as he's forced to tell me the truth. Forced to tell me what I already know. He hasn't been faithful.

I need him to say it. I need him to admit to it. I need to know why.

I already know the answers to all of it.

It's because we don't have a family. It's because I'm not well. It's because I let myself go physically.

He's tired of being with someone like me.

I feel a tear welling in my eye as I think about it all. Kev's arm shifts around my shoulder as he smiles at whatever's happening on the show. He finishes his slice and grabs another from the box. It's his third. I haven't managed to take more than a few bites of my first slice.

I take a deep breath. I need to know what's happening. I open my mouth, not knowing what will come out.

That's when I remember the letter. "Do not tell him or anybody else about this letter. OR ELSE."

This isn't some prank. Teenagers didn't make it.

The person who wrote me that letter spoke of consequences. I have no doubt they mean it.

Somehow, I know this won't end with strange knocks at my door.

That doesn't mean I can't get answers. I smile to myself as I think of the perfect solution. A way to force answers from Kevin about the second cell without telling him about the letter.

"Be right back," I say to him.

"You want me to pause?" Kev asks.

In my haste to follow through with my plan, I don't answer. Instead, I head up the stairs, my cell phone ready. I dial Kevin's second phone number again, ensuring I use star six nine before I do.

I don't care how much the service costs; it will be worth it when I come back downstairs.

I don't mess around. As my cell phone calls Kevin's second cell, I grab the actual cell phone from the bottom drawer of his nightstand.

It's time to get answers. I let my cell phone ring many times before disconnecting the call. I slip my cell in my jogging pants pocket. Gripping Kevin's second phone tightly, I slowly make my way back down the stairs until I enter the living room.

He looks at me with a smile on his face. "You're missing some good drama," he says. "Kelly just dumped Jason. You—"

"What's this?" I say, showing him his second phone. I don't need any more fake drama in my life. I have very real situations happening.

When Kevin realizes what I'm holding, his smile quickly vanishes.

CHAPTER 13

I hold out the second cell, waiting for his response. I pictured this going differently. Him stumbling over his words, pleading for forgiveness for what he's done.

Instead, he just gawks at me oddly. "What?" he finally says.

"What is this?" I say with a harsher tone.

He lets out an anxious laugh, dropping the rest of his slice on the pizza box. "It's my cell phone," he says.

Finally, he admits to something. "Why do you have a second cell phone, Kev?" I demand. I take a step forward, the proof still gripped in my hand. "I heard it buzzing. You were hiding it in your dresser. Why?"

He shakes his head. "Hiding?" He stands up from the couch and takes a step towards me. His bright blue eyes turn dark as he gets closer. For a moment, I see something in him I have never seen before. An anger that changes his whole demeanour.

He must have noticed how his reaction scared me and gives a thin smile. "I'm not hiding anything," he says. "Thats just my work phone."

"Since when have you had a work phone?" I say, confused.

"It's a new thing," he says. He reaches out his hand and opens his palm to me. After a long moment, I place the cell in his hand.

"You never told me about getting a work phone," I say, confused.

"Yeah," he says. "Well, I have one. What's the big deal, Jo?"

I think of the letter that's hiding under the couch.

"I'm surprised you wouldn't have told me about your work phone," I say, confidently. "Wouldn't you want me to have the number too to call you in case of an emergency or something?"

He laughs. "I don't even know the number to it."

I do, I think to myself, but don't share that information.

"I haven't even set up the voicemail on it yet," he says with a smile. "How did you find it?"

"Some random number tried to call you," I say. "I heard it vibrating in the bedroom."

"You heard it?" he says. He opens the cell. "It looks like someone called with a private number." He shakes his head. "I need to set up the voicemail." He looks at me. "If it's important, they'd have called me on my regular cell."

I stare at him, examining his face and expression for clues he's lying. All I see is his beautiful eyes and gorgeous face staring back at me. Suddenly, he furrows his eyebrows and scowls at me.

"Why are you so upset about this?" he asks. "What did you think you found? It's just a cell."

I lower my head. The answer to the question is hiding under the pizza and couch cushion behind him. I remember the threat the letter said.

"I don't know what I thought," I say, confused. "It just doesn't make sense."

"Me having a work phone doesn't make sense?" he

repeats. When he says it so plainly, I feel stupid.

I have a right to be worried though. The letter left at my door is telling me something is wrong.

"Who messaged you last week?" I ask. I feel my heartbeat faster and weak at the knees.

His facial features harden. "This again?" he says. "This is what I get." He scoffs. "I wanted to talk to you today about our anniversary. Did you forget about it?"

"No, I haven't," I say with a tone. "Of course not."

"Well, I wanted to talk to you about it tonight. How can I now? Not while you're doing this to me."

"What?" I say. I'm the one who's confused. I'm the one who has questions.

"You're accusing me of the worst things, Jo." He shakes his head. "How could you think I would be this type of husband to you? Never!" He takes a step back and puts a hand to his head. "I would never break our vow. I've been with you through everything. Everything! We lost our child. I was there for you. I've been here through all your ups and downs."

"You have," I say, taking a step towards him.

He shrugs. "No," he says. "You wouldn't be like this if you thought well of me. You don't trust me, and for the life of me, I don't know why."

I feel my body loosen. Suddenly, I'm guilt-stricken by what I'm doing, until I remember the text message from last week.

"Who messaged you, Kev?" I say again. "Why are you hiding who it is? Why can't you just tell me?"

He shakes his head. "And why can't you just trust me?" When I don't answer, he takes out his other cell phone from his pocket. With both cells in his hands, he stares at me. "What will it take for you to believe your husband is a good man?"

"Kev, I—"

"No!" he shouts. His face is full of rage for a moment but instantly softens. "I guess this is our marriage now. This is how it is." He unlocks his primary phone, followed by the second. With a phone in each hand, he reaches towards me. "Go ahead."

"Kev," I plead.

"No," he says. "Go ahead. You don't trust me. You want to know who texted me. Look for yourself. Go ahead."

I'm tempted to reach out first for his primary phone to read the text message. Why can't he just tell me? After that, I'd grab the work phone to see if there are any text messages and who's been calling.

With the look on his face, I know this is a test, though. If I grab either of those phones, there will be consequences.

"I trust you," I say. "It's just confusing."

He nods his head towards his phone. "No matter what I say, you won't believe it, right? I'm such a liar. A terrible liar. A no-good husband, right? So, why would you listen to anything I have to say? Find out for yourself." He takes a step towards me, the phones getting closer.

"Stop, Kev," I plead. I lower my head, and wave him to get the phones out of my face. "I trust you."

He lowers his hands and scoffs. "You trust me?" he repeats with a tone. "I need you to start showing me that you trust me, Jo." When I don't answer, he shakes his head. "What's wrong with our marriage? What's wrong with us?" He looks at me, his bright blue eyes striking my soul with his words. "What's wrong with you?"

CHAPTER 14

I lie in bed, staring at the ceiling. Tonight was rough. After our argument, we ended our pizza and reality television date. He went to our bedroom. I paced around the house, trying to think of what to say to make it better.

I thought about showing him the letter. Anybody would question their husband if they found a letter like that outside their house.

After a while, I went to our bedroom, and to my surprise, Kev was already sleeping. It wasn't even eight at night, and he was sound asleep. I heard his deep breathing and random snorts.

I knew he wasn't faking it to not speak to me. Part of me wanted to wake him to talk about what happened. I shouldn't have taken so much time downstairs. I was too busy trying to process everything.

It's too late now. He's asleep. Feeling defeated, I slip into the sheets. I stare at the ceiling, wondering how to recover from this.

Nothing makes sense.

Part of me wishes I just grabbed his cell phones. I could have quelled my anxieties by finding out the truth.

Kev's right, though. If I grabbed them, I would only prove how much I don't trust him. Why would you stay married to a person you can't trust?

The problem isn't Kev. It's my mistrust. It's my own insecurities. It's me.

I need to trust my husband. Even if I looked at his cell phones, maybe I'd feel better at the time, finding out nothing was going on behind my back, but the next time something fishy happened, I'd spiral again.

That's not how marriage is supposed to work.

I'm supposed to be open and honest with my husband. I shouldn't have kept the heart-shaped letter from him. A normal person would have likely told their spouse about it immediately.

Part of me thinks the anonymous person who wrote it is on my side. They're trying to show me something. Why, though?

As my mind runs a mile a minute, Kev turns over and looks at me. I'm surprised he's not sleeping. I wonder how long he's been awake for.

"Hey," I say softly.

He doesn't respond. In the dark, I can see him purse his lips. "We need to talk," he says.

I nearly gasp. That's not how you start a good conversation.

This is it. This is the moment that changes my life forever. What did I expect? Of course he's going to break up with me. The next few words will confirm it.

He wants a divorce. It makes sense. After how I reacted in the living room tonight, how could he want to stay with a woman like me?

He moves his head so it's closer to mine. "I love you," he says. He reaches out and grabs my hip. "I love you, Josie," he says again. "You know that, right?"

I'm already nearly in tears as he says the words. It's exactly what I needed to hear. It's almost like he read my mind and could tell how insecure I was.

"I'm sorry," I say, nearly whispering.

"I need you to trust me, Jo," he says, caressing my hips. "I need that. The rest of the world can burn, but I need my wife to trust me, okay?"

I nod my head and turn to him. "Okay," I say. "I'm sorry, Kev."

He smiles. "It's okay. I know it's been tough. But someday you'll be the mother of my children."

He's saying it again. Last time we fought, he brought up having kids. What if I can't? What if I'm too scared to attempt it? I'm nearly a type two diabetic now. My body's changed and it feels like it won't ever look like how it did before I was pregnant.

"Kev, what if it doesn't happen?" I ask. "What if I can't give you a child?"

He smiles again. "You'll see," he says. "No matter what, everything will be okay. What happened wasn't because of your diabetes. You're a good woman, Jo. That's why I fell in love with you. I never met someone like you before. You're special. Whatever happens, we'll be okay." He kisses my forehead and turns and looks up at the ceiling. "I was going to go out with the guys after work tomorrow, if that's okay?"

I sigh. Here we go. Now, he thinks he needs permission to do things with friends. "Of course it is," I say.

He turns and looks at me. "Isn't tomorrow your bar night with your friends? I think you should go."

I'm surprised he's encouraging me to go out. Last time I mentioned the bar, he got so upset, even bringing up that Trey would be there as a reason why he didn't like the idea.

"Okay," I say. "Thanks." I'm not sure why I thank him, but he smiles at me.

Maybe I'm just happy that he woke up and talked to me. Never go to bed angry. It's the one thing I always pride myself on with Kev.

He looks back at the ceiling. "You know what's weird? I could have sworn I put my work phone on silent." He takes a deep breath and turns away from me.

CHAPTER 15

I sit in my cubicle, thinking about everything that's happened. I think about my crazy behaviour lately and the talk I had with Kev last night. Anytime I start to feel better and calm my anxiety, I think about the mysterious letter I found.

It's still under my couch cushion at home. Kevin left early this morning. I went back and forth about telling him about it after our talk. I want to believe all the nice things he said to me in bed. I want to believe him, but who sent the letter? Why did this person send it?

I thought if I showed him the letter, he could understand why I was so out of it yesterday when I found the second phone.

I should just throw the letter away. This morning, I had many opportunities to do so. I could have easily tossed it, burnt it or given it to Q to play with and destroy. Instead, I pretended it didn't exist and left it under the cushion.

I imagine Kev coming home early from work only to discover it. That would be another awkward night, and I don't think I have the energy for that.

Besides, Kevin's going out tonight with his friends from work. Of course, I know that means Stacy Wingham will be joining them. I never thought I'd be the type of person to get so jealous of my husband having a female friend. I just wish she was an ugly female friend. I'm sure that would be easier to stomach.

Not the case with Stacy.

"Working hard I see, McNeil," a booming voice says behind me. I turn and Mr. Dunstrow is staring at me with his head tilted and a look of general unpleasantness on him. Unfortunately, this is his normal face though, so it's hard to tell if I'm in trouble or not.

"Morning, Mr. Dunstrow," I say, managing a smile.

He nods without a friendly gesture back. "We have quarterly stats coming up soon. Remember to keep your call volume up, okay?"

"No problem," I say. He gives me a thin smile but doesn't say another word. There's an awkward pause until he moves on to bother another cubicle and the person inside it.

I shake my head, annoyed. I seriously hate this job. Terrible calls. A terrible boss. If it wasn't for the decent employees, I'd join the many who quit before me.

I like to think I'd have the courage to quit, but I'd be too scared. Unless I had another job lined up, it would be hard for me to put in notice to leave Nexen Power.

Besides, to get a job you need references, and my company has a policy of not giving them to employees. It's almost like you're trapped here. The longer you stay, the harder it is to leave.

Maybe a terrible call with another customer is just what I need to get my mind off my personal life. I won't have to think about my husband, the letter I received and all the terrible thoughts I've been having. I pick up my headphones, ready to tackle a call, turning to face my computer. Suddenly a knock on the side of my cubicle frame makes me turn.

Instantly, I know it's not Mr. Dunstrow. He never knocks. He'd rather awkwardly yell at the back of my head and make me wonder how long he's been standing outside my cubicle for.

Amber greets me when I turn my chair around. "Good morning," she says.

"Morning," I reluctantly say back, refusing to call it good by any means.

"What's up? Why the long face?"

I sigh. "Last night was so terrible."

"Why?" she asks. "I thought you said things have been better the last week."

"They were," I say. Without thinking, I tell her part of the truth. "I found out that Kev has a second phone." I shake my head. "All that talk from you about how cheaters have second phones made me so anxious."

"Oh, I'm so sorry, Jo," she says, wrapping her arm around my shoulder. "I always knew he was a piece of trash. He doesn't deserve someone like you."

I'm surprised by her reaction. She's never referred to him that way. I'm sure she's trying to support me, though.

I take another deep breath. "It was his work phone," I say, covering my face. "I can't believe how I reacted. When I found the phone, I freaked out, thinking the worst. Kev has a new work phone. He never mentioned it before, though. He doesn't even have voicemail attached to it." I look at Amber, waiting for her to tell me the obvious. She doesn't fail me.

"Well, Jo, how do you know that it's a work phone if he doesn't have a voicemail?" She looks at me with an endearing gaze. When I glance back, she knows her words are hurting me. "Sorry, Jo. I'm just worried about you."

"I don't know what to believe sometimes. Kev got really upset when I showed him the second phone and I confronted him about it." I take another deep breath. "He unlocked both his personal cell and work one and told me to look at whatever I wanted."

Amber raises an eyebrow. "Well, what did you find out?"

I let out a laugh. "I didn't look at the phones."

"What? Girl, come on."

I shake my head with an awkward smile. "You don't understand. If I picked up one of those phones, my marriage would be over. Why would he unlock his phone if he has something to hide?" I glance at Amber and lower my head. "He's upset and he has every right to be. His wife is sneaking around, getting phone records and now, more accusations."

Amber purses her lips. "How did you find the phone?"

I shake my head, knowing that it was dumb of me to overshare. That's an obvious question to follow-up with after what I said.

I can see the frightening letter I found outside my door in my mind. I see the blocky cut out letters that made the shocking words.

"That's a bit of a story," I say.

Amber looks at me, confused. "What does that mean?"

I should have told Kev last night about the letter. Me staying quiet is giving this random person power over me by scaring me into silence.

"Someone left a letter outside my door last night," I say, glancing at Amber and looking away. "They rang my doorbell, and when I opened the door, nobody was there.

That's when I found the letter."

Amber looks shocked. "What? What did it say?"

I don't have to think too hard to remember. The words have been ingrained in my brain since reading it. I tell her word for word what it said.

Amber shakes her head. "So the number belonging to Kevin's second cell was from the letter?"

I nod. "I called the number on the letter and confronted Kev about it." I glance back at Amber, who still looks shocked and confused. Somehow, that helps me feel better.

"Did you tell Kev about the letter?" she asks.

I shake my head. "I was too scared to." I take a deep breath. "Tonight I will, though. I'll show it to him."

"This is weird," she says.

Understatement of the century.

I let out an anxious laugh. "You know what else is weird? Kev says he put his work phone on silent. That makes me wonder."

"Wonder what?" she asks.

"Did whoever left me the letter come into my house and turn the phone off silent so I could find it?"

Amber looks at me strangely. "You don't just tell Kev about the letter, Jo. You need to call the police."

Before I can answer, Trey walks into my cubicle. "Did you say police?" he asks, confused. "Letter?"

I look at Amber, who understands not to say a word. "It's nothing," I say.

"Just talking about a show we're watching," Amber says, coming in with a solid white lie.

He nods. "Bar night tonight. Count you girls in?"

Amber looks at me.

"I'll be going," I say. Amber nods and says she will

too.

"Perfect." He looks behind him and back at us, his eyes full of expression. "Mr. Dunstrow's on the prowl. Time to escape back to my cubicle." He leaves quickly.

I expect Amber to do the same, but instead, she stares at me. "This is weird, Jo," she says. "Scary stalker weird."

CHAPTER 16

The rest of the workday goes by at a snail's pace. All I can think about is Amber's reaction to what happened. She's genuinely worried about the letter at my door. I didn't even mention how the letters that made up the words were cut out from a newspaper.

After my whirlwind of a night with Kev, I'm too exhausted to really process it all.

This isn't normal. I think about calling the police. What would I even say? The truth, obviously, but how would an officer respond?

I doubt they'll take it seriously to the point of checking for fingerprints or testing for DNA. I'll tell them about the weird letter, and they'll look back at me, confused as to why they should care.

Yes, it's odd, but not exactly a crime.

When I get to our driveway, I take my time parking inside. We have a two-car garage with no connecting door into our house. Despite being made for two vehicles, there's very little space left with just one car parked.

Kev jokes that I just don't know how to park a car. "Plenty of space," he always jests. He's even used a permanent marker to help me line up my parking better. I think it's fine, but he's just too type A.

Today, I couldn't care less. I park and get out of my

car and close the garage behind me before walking up the steps of the front porch.

When will Kev come home tonight? After speaking with Amber, I feel the need to tell him everything. The first thing I'll do is take the letter out from underneath the couch cushion.

No more pretending it doesn't exist. It's time to take whoever left me this letter more seriously. Someone has it in for me, or is it Kev?

It's all so confusing. I turn my key and unlock the door. I gently push it open and when I do, a heart-shaped letter reveals itself at my feet. On top of the indoor mat inside our house is a second message.

In bold cut-out letters, the words mock me. "READ ME NOW."

CHAPTER 17

I look at the cut-out letters on the front. The letter was inside my house. Whoever left it was inside my house.

My arm goes limp as I look around. Nothing seems out of place. Even Q doesn't seem that alarmed. She leaps off the couch and brushes against my leg, greeting me. If only I got a dog, maybe this wouldn't have happened. A big, vicious dog.

When I look at Q's face, I instantly forgive her lack of securing my house. With Q comforting me, I let go of a breath I didn't know I was holding.

Part of me wants to grab Q, run outside my house and call the police. The other part can't help but read what's inside. I reluctantly open the letter.

"He's cheating on you."

As I read the words, I take a deep breath. I feel my heart sink inside my chest as I continue to read.

"He's bringing her to your house tonight. Tell NOBODY about this letter or there will be consequences."

I reread the letter a few times, the words feeling more painful. I take a deep breath, realizing this is ridiculous.

Whoever sent me this letter knows what Kevin is doing. They know he plans to bring a woman to our house tonight. How?

Someone who knows Kev is trying to ruin our marriage. Or help me discover the truth.

It hits me. Kev asked me last night if I was planning on going out after work. I told him I was. If he's having an affair, why would he even think about bringing her back to our house? A house he shares with his wife? Pictures of us surround me. Whatever woman he brings here, if he even does, would see the same memories that I do now.

It's ridiculous.

Yet an anonymous person went out of their way to tell me it's not. They left a letter saying my husband is cheating.

Instead of feeling scared or sad, I feel rage inside me. Why are they taunting me this way? Why would they leave me letters that scare me half to death? Now, they've broken into my home and left me with another surprise.

I storm into the kitchen. Just as in the living room, nothing seems out of place. I go to the back door and open it. To my surprise, it's unlocked. My mouth opens as I realize that's how they got inside. The person who left me the letter was inside my house and came through the back door.

Did I leave it unlocked?

When I open the back door fully, I step outside and look around, shocked. Who's doing this to me? Why are they doing this to me?

I want it all to stop.

What if they're telling the truth? What if Kevin hasn't been faithful? I still don't know who texted him last week. He refuses to tell me.

When I look around the edge of my house, I see the back gate that leads to the front of the house is open. I know for certain that I didn't use the gate.

I take out my cell phone.

No more games. Whoever's doing this broke into my house. As I quickly dial nine and one, I hesitate.

After all the arguments with Kevin, my brain won't let up that something is off in our relationship. With the arguments I've been having with my husband, I felt that it was just me.

What would happen if instead of going out tonight, I stay in? What if I didn't go out as Kev expected me to? When he comes home, will he be by himself, as expected? Or is the letter right?

I step inside and close the back door, ensuring it's locked.

If I did stay home, I couldn't keep my car in the garage. If I did, Kev would see it immediately. I quickly go out the front door, grabbing my keys along the way. It's almost as if I'm possessed. I don't feel like I'm inside my body, controlling what I'm doing. It's almost as if a third person has taken over as I get into my car, drive several blocks away and park.

As I quickly walk back to my house, I wonder what I'm doing. It's a stupid question because I know exactly why I'm doing this.

Is he cheating? As much as I trust Kevin and want to believe him, I can't help but think something is wrong in our marriage. It's not just the long hours and time away from him either.

Something else is wrong. That's why I've been so off. I can almost feel the tension when he's around. It's as if my body knows something is wrong but my brain is trying to catch up, trying to come up with rational reasons why I feel this way.

I've never been the clingy type of woman. A woman who needs to know where their partner is at all times. I've never been the jealous type either.

My mantra is I need to trust my partner and if they break that trust, leave them. But I feel like, with Kev, I'm going insane with jealousy and clinginess.

As I step back inside my house, I wonder how crazy this is. The other side of me knows it's too late. I tidy up the living room. I don't know why. It's almost as if I'm cleaning up for an unexpected guest.

This is stupid. I should go out. No, I should contact the police. Someone broke into my house and left a letter telling me my husband is cheating. I think of the words inside. They continue to give me warnings about not telling anyone.

I remember the first letter under the couch. I quickly lift the cushion. When I see it, I wonder what to do with it. Part of me wants to burn them for how crazy I feel.

I take a deep breath. This could be all one cruel prank. If Kevin comes home alone, I'll know that this is all it is. I'll show him the letters.

If I call the police, I'll never get to find out if the letter was right. I'll never find out the truth.

Taking the first letter, I go back to the kitchen, where the second is waiting for me on the table. With both letters in my hand, I look at them, unable to understand why this is happening to me.

I take a deep breath and try to catch up to my thoughts. I'm supposed to be leaving by now to go to the bar. Amber will be wondering where I am.

How do I even explain this to her?

I take out my cell phone and start to text her. "Hey, I can't make it tonight." For a moment, I think about telling her why. She knows about the first letter. Now that I found a second letter inside my house, the ominous warning frightens me more.

"Tell NOBODY about this letter or there will be consequences." I can't get the words from the letter out of my brain.

I finish my text message. "I'm not feeling well. Just going to stay in. Sorry."

I send the message and get a reply almost immediately. "Come out, Jo," Amber pleads. I can almost hear her concern for me. "I can't stop thinking about what you said today about that weird letter. It really freaked me out. Are you home alone?"

If I told Amber about the second letter and how I found it inside my house, she'd tell me to immediately call the police. She would be right.

It's what the letters say that stops me. It's my own need to find out the truth that makes me follow through with what the letter wants me to do.

"I'm okay," I reply. "Kev will be home soon."

I shake my head as I send the message. He will be at some point. The question is, will he be alone?

The other question is, where do I hide? If Kev's having an affair, the obvious place he'd bring her is the bedroom. The idea makes me sick. My stomach turns at the thought of my husband in our marriage bed with someone else.

Whoever sent this letter knows something I don't. They're trying to show me the truth. It's time I see it for myself.

When I open the bedroom door, I look at our marriage bed. Kevin wouldn't do that to me. He would never bring a woman to our bedroom. Yet I close the door behind me. I open the closet and step inside. I feel foolish as I slide the closet door closed behind me.

What am I doing with my life? I'm hiding in closets to find out if my husband is cheating on me. I can't stop a tear from forming as I sit on the carpeted floor. I spread my fingers in the long fibers. It weirdly soothes me.

I hear noise coming from outside the bedroom door. I freeze in place, my fingers gripping the carpet fabric. When I hear Q's paws on the bedroom door, I let out a breath.

If ever there would be a dead giveaway that I'm home, it's Q waiting outside the bedroom door. I open the door and pick her up.

"You must be quiet," I tell her as I close the closet door behind us. I pet her and remind her to keep her loud purring at a minimum. It's not easy to negotiate with a cat, though.

Thankfully, she's calming me. Q is much nicer to pet than the carpet. I start to think about what I'm doing. Every time I consider leaving, or how stupid I feel, I think about the letter and what it said.

The first letter told me about the second cell phone Kev has. It wasn't lying. So, was Kevin lying?

I could call his work and find out if they gave out phones to employees. I'm not sure how I could ask without coming off like a maniac. Maybe I could say I'm trying to get a hold of Kev and he's not picking up his regular phone. I'll say I know he has a work phone but don't have the number.

As I come up with more ways to discover if Kev is being truthful, I think about our argument the other night. I see my husband's face as I accuse him of being unfaithful. I could see the pain in his eyes when I showed him the second phone and demanded answers.

I open the closet door hard and look at Q.

"What am I doing?" I ask her. "What have I become?"

As my thoughts run wild, I hear the front door open. I hear a voice downstairs. A laugh. I instantly recognize Kevin's voice. What I don't recognize is the giggle of the woman who's with him.

CHAPTER 18

The letter was right, again!
Kev brought a woman home with him. He actually has a girl downstairs in our house. I can hear the muffled sounds of them.
I'm in shock as I hear them laugh again. What could be so funny? I imagine opening the bedroom door and storming downstairs to confront them.
Who's with him?
Some floozy from the bar? I think of the text message from last week. I'm about to interrupt their "fun".
I'm paralyzed as I hear them downstairs. I feel my heart beat quicker in my chest. I could have a heart attack and die before I ever discover who the woman downstairs is. Needing to know the truth, I reach out and lean on the mattress. I sit on it and try to calm my nerves. Q jumps on my lap and tries to help.
It hits me. Any minute, the two of them will come up stairs and enter this bedroom. I spread my finger across the fabric of the bedsheets. Any moment, he'll enter this room with her and stain these sheets with his adultery.
Only, I don't hear them coming up. Instead, I hear them continue to talk downstairs. Their muffled voices

sound happy. I don't know what they're saying but my imagination is already making up every situation and none of them end with it being a visit from a platonic friend.

Kev laughs again, almost confirming what's happening downstairs is playful banter leading up to one thing.

My life is over. I imagine being single in my thirties. I imagine having to tell my mom that I'm divorcing Kev. I can only imagine the pity in her voice as she finds out what he did.

I imagine whoever sent the letter to me finding out the same. Will they be happy? Whoever's leaving the messages for me wanted this to happen. Well, here it is. It's all led up to this.

I thought I wanted to know the truth. What if I continued being happy with Kev and didn't ruin the facade? Maybe life would have been better if I never knew what he was doing.

I know that's not true, though. I know I'm just prolonging what I have to do.

I need to confront them. I need to see who she is.

Standing up from the bed, Q jumps off my lap. I take a deep breath and quietly open the bedroom door. Their voices become clearer as I do.

"Before we start," Kev says with a charming tone, "how does a glass of wine sound?"

"You read my mind," the woman says back playfully.

Oh God. What is happening? I feel a tear run down the side of my face.

While I was preparing for this moment, I thought about what I would say if a woman did come back home with Kevin. As I walked back to my house after parking my car blocks away, I imagined in my head what I would do. I'd point at the woman and call her a homewrecker, a slut. A few times, I imagined striking her in the face.

As I take another step, the stair creaks. I stop. That's not how this is going to go down. Tears are running freely down my face now as I get closer to the living room. I take my time with the final few stairs as the woman in my living room is in sight. Well, most of her. She's wearing a tight white skirt and black blouse. As I take a final step, I finally see her face.

Stacy Wingham smiles, her long legs crossed. Her silky thigh bounces on her knee with anticipation, until she sees me.

Her face drops. Kevin enters the living room from the kitchen with two wineglasses in his hands. His smile quickly vanishes as he notices me.

"Jo?" he says, surprised.

CHAPTER 19

"What are you doing here?" he says, confused. He continues across the living room and hands Stacy the wineglass.

Stacy hasn't looked away from me. She sees the tears. She recognizes that I know what they're up to. She places the glass on the living room table where a few folders and binders take up most of the surface.

"I knew it was you," I say to Stacy. I feel a tear drop from the tip of my chin. "I knew it. Are you having *fun* now?"

Between my sobs, I feel my anger rising. I could kill her right now. Take one of those heavy looking binders and strike her as hard as I could. It would feel glorious.

Kev steps closer to me. "What are you doing?"

I ignore his question. "I want to know what you two are doing," I say.

Kev waves his hand. "Working, Jo." He nods towards the table and the paperwork.

Stacy doesn't say a word and continues to look at me, confused.

"No, you're not," I say.

I know it can't be. The letter told me Kev would bring a woman home. And that woman is his stupid work wife, Stacy. I knew it. It should have been so easy to tell from the beginning.

I realize that must be why her text message didn't show as a saved number on his phone last week. She must have sent it from her work phone.

Kev lowers his head. "Lets just call it a night, Stacy." When he raises his head, he looks at his colleague.

Stacy glances at me and back at him. "Okay."

"I'm sorry," he says, fully turning to her. Stacy starts to gather the paperwork on the table. "I don't even know what to say."

"It's okay." She hurries to collect the rest.

I watch them, my mouth gaping open, tears still rolling down my face. I can only imagine how I look. Stacy looks gorgeous. Her perfume smells sweet like candy. Meanwhile, I must look like a sweaty mess from hiding upstairs for so long, a bunch of Q's hair clinging to my pants.

I don't know what to say as I continue to watch Kev guide Stacy to the front door. Before she leaves, I hear a small exchange.

"Are you going to be okay?" Stacy asks.

"I'm sorry," Kev repeats. "I'll be fine."

"This is worse than you told me," she says. "She looks cra—"

"Stop." Kev opens the front door. Stacy gazes at my husband a moment before leaving. "See you tomorrow," Kev says as he watches her go to her car. He lowers his head, closing the door slowly. After what feels like forever, he turns to me.

I don't know how to describe the look on his face. It's beyond words. I can see how angry he is. How much he hates me. I see all the resentments he's been holding onto. All the disappointments. He truly hates me.

Finally, he speaks. "Where's your car?" he says. "It wasn't in the garage." He squints as he looks at me for an answer. Instead of answering, I freeze at his rageful gaze.

CHAPTER 20

I never do answer Kev about where I parked my car. When I don't say a word, Kev goes up the stairs and slams the bedroom door shut. I hear him push the lock button on the door.

I sleep on the couch that night. Kev never comes out of our bedroom. I wait, hoping he will. The last few arguments we had, we were able to talk after and resolve it.

Never go to bed angry.

Well, I'm not on the bed. I'm on the couch. The doghouse, as they say.

I never thought Kev would force me to sleep on the couch. He must be so disgusted with me that he doesn't want to look at me. His crazy wife has embarrassed him again. Only this time there was an audience.

Hearing Stacy call me crazy before leaving our house was just the cherry on top. *Crazy?* That's exactly how I feel. The letters I've received and thoughts of infidelity swarming inside me have made me utterly insane.

After failing to sleep for over an hour, tossing and turning on the couch, I stare at the ceiling. I want a clear answer on what's happening. Why is someone leaving letters? Why can't I trust my husband?

The faint smell of Stacy's perfume reminds me. I'm forced to sleep on the same couch where all this mess happened tonight.

How much worse can this get? I already know the answer. I know how this story ends. Divorce.

Kev's going to leave me.

I think about knocking on our bedroom door but know that will make things worse. He clearly wants space from his crazy wife.

I think of Stacy. I smell her perfume. Who wouldn't want a woman like her?

I think about what the two will say to each other at work tomorrow. They seemed to giggle it up tonight at our house before I entered the picture.

I picture her at the watercooler asking Kevin if his nutty wife is less crazy today. I imagine them laughing it up at how embarrassing tonight was.

Staring wide-eyed at the ceiling, I know that I won't be sleeping anytime soon tonight. I slip out of the comforter and head into the kitchen, opening the pantry. I dig in the back of a shelf until I find the small container I'm looking for. Several gummy worms are inside it. I gobble them quickly, hoping to find relief in the high sugar content.

That's when I hear a noise outside. A scratching sound of metal. I realize it's the gate.

My eyes widen at the sound. I turn on the lights outside my house. Nobody is outside, at least as far as I can tell. When I open the back door, my heart flutters in my chest. Then suddenly, I hear a car engine. Barefoot, I step outside and see the metal gate swinging open. A sleek red sports car is idling, then slowly passes by.

CHAPTER 21

I sit in my cubicle, staring at the screen. I may be at work, but I'm not present. I'm not here whatsoever. I haven't even turned on my computer. I can't. I feel frozen. I wish I wasn't here. I wish last night didn't happen.

First, I found a second letter. Then I hid. Kev came home with Stacy, and I embarrassed myself, worse than before.

Then there was whatever happened in my backyard late last night. I thought I heard the gate open. When I went outside, though, nobody was there. Did I shut the gate when I went into the backyard after finding the second letter? Or was whoever doing this to me in my backyard last night? Did going into the kitchen last night scare someone who was hiding outside?

Was that their red car I saw? Do I ever wish I was a car girl. It makes me think of Trey and the sports car calendar he has in his cubicle. I wonder if I describe the red car I saw last night to him, would he know the make of the car?

I take a deep breath, unsure what to do.

Kev left the house this morning. He took a moment and glanced at me on the couch before leaving. Before I could say a word, he left. He didn't greet me. He didn't say anything.

How did my life get to this?

My marriage is burning in front of me. The person leaving me the letters is only adding more gasoline to the fire.

I come out of my daze when I feel like someone is watching me. When I turn, Trey greets me.

"Thought you were going to come out last night," he says.

I look at him, unsure what to say. "Something came up."

He looks at me with concern. I'm not sure what someone who's mentally breaking down looks like, but I'm sure I'm close to that image.

Suddenly, Amber enters my cubicle as well. I let out a deep breath. I should have called in sick. In fact, I should have called the police. I should be explaining to Kev why I'm this way.

I wish my cubicle had a door I could shut today.

Amber takes one look at me and her entire face softens. I must look worse than I feel.

"What happened last night?" she asks. "I was worried when you didn't come out."

A lot happened last night. A second letter. Me hiding in my own house and catching my husband and his hot coworker, working, with a glass of wine. It's all so innocent yet feels wrong. I'm not sure who to believe.

Was I wrong for accusing my husband, again, of cheating? Am I the villain for embarrassing him in front of Stacy? After what happened last night, I certainly feel like the bad guy.

I let out a heavy breath. No. Whoever left the letter inside my house is the real villain.

"Tell no one," the letter said. Amber already knows

about the first letter, but for some reason, I keep the discovery of the second one to myself.

"Just a night in with Kevin," I say. My answer doesn't reassure them, it seems, as they both stare at me. "We had another fight." I lower my head. "It wasn't a good night."

Trey and Amber exchange a look.

"Did you fight because of the letter?" Trey asks.

I look shocked when he said the words and immediately look at Amber.

She looks at me innocently. "Sorry," she says. "He heard you talking about the letter the other day. Last night at the bar, I may have opened up to him about it more than I should have."

"It's okay," Trey says. "I'm sure you were scared when you found the letter. What did Kevin say when you told him about it?"

I glance at him again before lowering my head in defeat. "We didn't fight about that."

"What was it about?" Trey asks. His questioning starts to annoy me. It's none of his damn business. I'm not going to tell him that my marriage is breaking down, that I can't stop thinking my husband is cheating on me. I can't tell him that every time I call Kevin out, he has the perfect excuse.

I can't tell if I'm being gaslighted or losing my mind. Add on top of that, an anonymous person is sending me letters, and I know my entire life is breaking down.

"I don't want to talk about it," I say.

Trey catches the hint and doesn't ask more questions about Kevin. He does, however, give me an unwelcome opinion.

"Sorry," he says. "I guess I'm just thinking, what if whoever's sending you these letters is trying to help you?"

"Help me?" I say, surprised. I look at Amber. I wonder how much she told him. Did she mention the cut-up letters that make the words inside? Did she share the warnings?

Of course they don't know about the second letter. If she knew, Amber would drive me to the police station immediately.

Trey looks at me, pursing his lips. "I mean, it sounds like this person is trying to show you something about Kevin. Something that you don't know."

I shake my head. "I don't want to know any more. I just want to forget the whole thing."

Trey's about to say something, likely more unwelcome opinions on the anonymous letters, when Mr. Dunstrow walks up and joins us outside my cubicle.

"Company meeting?" he asks with a tone. He doesn't wait for one of us to answer his rhetorical question. "Back to your cubicles, please."

Trey and Amber do as asked. Mr. Dunstrow stands outside mine. He looks at my computer monitor that's still turned off. When he meets my eyes, his expression is full of disappointment.

"Josie," he says, "I think you and I need to have a conversation." He clears his throat. "The tardiness lately and job performance has me quite concerned."

I'm so close to telling him what I really want to say. Instead, I bite my lip. "Okay."

CHAPTER 22

What a day.

The meeting I had with Mr. Dunstrow turned into an official disaster with one of the ladies from human resources sitting in. Mr. Dunstrow chewed me out for being late and for a list of other infractions I wasn't aware he was even keeping track of. I've been put on an official performance plan. In all my time at Nexen Power, I've never had these types of work issues before.

I've known a few coworkers who were put on a performance plan in the past. Usually, it's a one-way road to an eventual termination. The company's paved way to fire someone to lessen the chance of being sued afterwards for wrongful termination.

I'm very surprised it's happened to me. Who actually wants to work for Nexen? It's a revolving door of unhappy employees. I've put up with this place for so many years and this is what I get?

A performance plan.

I now have to meet with the HR woman once a week for the next month. Not only is my marriage falling apart, but it looks like I'll be needing to find a new job as well.

Perfect. Just perfect.

The rest of the workday went on as usual, which is pretty terrible on its own. I had a few nasty calls with unhappy customers. One called me several four-letter names. I hung up on them. There was only so much abuse I could stand today.

Amber didn't come back to my cubicle. Trey didn't ask for a game of cribbage. Things spread quickly at Nexen. The clear glass walls couldn't hide what happened with my meeting with HR and Mr. Dunstrow.

There's only one thing that's positive. It's the end of the workday. As I gather my things to leave, my cell buzzes on top of my desk. I let out a heavy breath when I see it's from Kevin.

I can't help but smile. He's texting me. We didn't talk last night. He didn't want to speak to me this morning. Now is our chance to finally resolve what happened.

Now I'll be forthcoming about everything that I've been keeping secret.

I quickly open the text.

"I'm not coming home tonight," his message reads. My heart sinks in my chest. "I need a break."

Break?

I don't have to ask who from. The answer is me. But does it mean our marriage? Does he want to separate? Does he mean he just needs more time before we speak? How can we resolve what happened if he doesn't want to talk?

I take a moment before I start my reply. "When will I see you?"

He responds immediately. "I don't know."

My arm slips to my side, my cell nearly dropping out of my hand. I lower my head, defeated. What have I done? How could I let my marriage get to this?

Our two-year anniversary is in a few days. We may not make it that long. I look around my cubicle. On one of the fake walls are a few pictures of Kev and me. All of them are happy moments captured over the years we've been together.

In the corner of my cubicle wall is the space left by a picture I removed months ago. It was the ultrasound image we had near the start of my second trimester.

This wasn't how my life was supposed to be. I wanted to be a mother. I wanted to have a family. Now, I may not even have a husband soon. I imagine that when Kevin finally does come around to talking to me, I'll be removing the rest of the pictures from this cubicle.

Well, I may not even have a cubicle, or this job, soon.

Who would have thought that the financial security of this terrible job would be something I'd want to cling to?

I take another deep breath and look at one of the lower cabinets. I bend and open it discreetly as if someone will catch me in the act. Sneaking out a bag of chips, I open it and take a single bite of one. I threw away most of the bad food I kept in my cubicle, except for this one bag. I thought I could use it as inspiration to stop eating crap. I liked rejecting it, but today it's too difficult to ignore.

I feel a wave of relief come over me as I eat more.

"That's right," the nasty voice inside me says, "eat more carbs. That solves everything."

I stop chewing, grab the small waste bin in my cubicle and spit out as much as I can. I hate this. I hate everything right now. I feel like I have nothing in my world that's safe. I could lose everything I have soon.

I need to leave here. I can't stay in my cubicle another moment, disgusted by how today went at work. Disgusted by how I walk around pitying myself.

I quickly make my way out of the building,

managing a quick smile for the security guard at the entrance. Her name is Tracy. She's been working security at the front entrance as long as I've been here. I remember when I interviewed for my position with Mr. Dunstrow, I was quite nervous waiting at the lobby for my interview. Tracy comforted me as I waited for him.

After being put on a performance plan, in a short time Tracy may have to guide me outside with a box of everything from my cubicle in my hands.

As I continue to think about the total disaster my life has become, I unlock my car and quickly get inside, turning on the ignition. What I need is to hibernate in my bedroom. I'm looking forward to being comforted by the only thing that won't leave me, Cutie Q.

That's when I see it. The edge of the heart-shaped letter flaps in the wind, most of it tucked into my wiper blade. I stare at it with disbelief.

I look around the parking lot, but nobody else is near me except for a few parked vehicles. I turn off my car and open the door. When I step outside and close the door, I notice something else. A long thick scratch starts from below my car hood and runs along the driver's side to the back.

I glance around the parking lot again, scared that the anonymous person is nearby. I know they aren't, though. It won't be that easy for me to figure out who it is.

I grab the heart-shaped letter from my windshield. As always, the front gives the same instructions.

"Read me. Now."

I let out a breath as I slowly open it to see what message they've made for me now.

"I warned you not to tell anyone."

CHAPTER 23

I'm sick and tired of this. I've had enough. No more games. I won't play with them anymore. I open the car door, throwing the letter in the backseat.

"What happened?" I turn and see Amber looking at my car. Trey's beside her and immediately comes up to it, feeling the scratch with his finger.

"That's deep," he says. He shakes his head. "This happened last month too. Remember that crazy guy whose power they cut off? Tracy from security literally had to chase him off the property." He stands up and stares at me. "Sorry, Jo. Do you have insurance for this?"

I don't answer his question. At this moment, I don't care. I'm more scared than angry.

Who's doing this?

I look at Trey, who bends over and examines the scratch again. When I turn, Amber is staring at me, her look of concern apparent.

How did the person sending me the letters know I told Amber? What happened to my car must be retribution for Trey and her knowing. How could that be possible?

Suddenly, Amber's look of worry seems fake. Trey's concern over my car seems just as ungenuine. My imagination runs wild with thoughts. Odd ones. What if it's one of them doing this to me?

Why, though?

How else could the letter writer know that I told Amber and Trey, unless it's one of them who's the culprit behind it all? I glance at Amber. Why is she even at work? She's usually off before me. She comes in early and goes home early. Not today though. Why?

Could she have put the letter on my windshield while at work?

I look around the near-empty lot. There are no security cameras on this side of the building. That's something employees have been complaining about for some time. The only cameras are focused on the front entrance and the limited spots for employees there. Most parking spots that are monitored with cameras are for customers.

Trey shakes his head. "Someone did a real number on your car."

Amber looks at me. "You told me Kev's ex scratched your car once."

I look at her and remember she's right. In my fear, I forgot entirely about the ordeal. Mary was so crazy after she found out Kev and I were engaged. A month later, I found a large scratch across on the hood of my car.

I always assumed it was Mary who did it but don't know for sure. But that scratch was tiny compared to this. This time the deep mark runs up the entire driver's side of my car.

Trey lets out a sigh. "Well, I'll go to the front desk and get Tracy. It's best to report this."

None of this makes sense. Now I'm getting letters at my work. The person sending me them knows I told my coworkers about the letter. How? Again, I look at Amber and Trey suspiciously.

I feel the urge to get away from my supposed friends as quickly as I can.

"Don't," I say. "I'll figure this out on my own."

Trey looks at me, confused. "Let's call the cops at the very least." He takes out his phone.

"Stop!" I shout. He looks surprised while Amber raises her eyebrows. I don't think either have heard me raise my voice before. Even when we have terrible phone calls with customers, I never shout back.

"I said I'll handle it." I open the car door and step inside, slamming it behind me.

CHAPTER 24

I sit in my house, the doors locked and drapes shut. Before relaxing on the couch with Q, I looked around each room. I don't know what I was expecting. It's not crazy to think who's ever doing this could have been in my house. They've been inside my house before.

I let out a nervous laugh as I opened the closet door in my bedroom, knowing that the other night I hid in here myself. When I got the second letter, I felt in my core that this time I would find out the truth. Whoever sent it was so specific. Kev is cheating, it said. A woman would show up at my house with my husband.

And sure enough, that's exactly what happened. Kev came home with Stacy.

After I found the third letter, my mind raced with crazy thoughts that perhaps it was Trey or even Amber that's behind them. How else could the anonymous person know about me telling Trey and Amber about the letters?

I sit on my couch. Q purrs on my chest as I pet her. Usually, I find it comforting lying with her. But all my mind can think about is figuring out who's ruining my life.

What would happen if I just called the police immediately? Part of me thinks about what Trey said.

What if this person sending letters to me is trying to help?

Why would someone threaten me the way the anonymous person is if they were truly friendly? Sure, because of the letters, I discovered a second cell phone, and just like the second letter said, Stacy came to my house with Kevin.

Stacy Wingham.

It would make a lot of sense for her to be behind the letters. Kev's work wife. What if she wants me out of the picture?

How could she do that? Make Kevin's real wife go insane with jealousy? She could send me letters, telling me things that make it seem like Kevin is cheating on me, even though she knows it's entirely innocent.

That makes a lot of sense.

No wonder Kevin's been so upset. He's done nothing wrong. Stacy would have known about the work phone. She would have received her own second phone herself. Stacy would have known she would be coming to my house the other night. She could have easily manipulated the situation with Kevin to come to our house to work.

There is, of course, the scratch on my car. Was Stacy at my work today? I remember what happened last night. I saw a red car drive away.

Last week, Stacy gave Kevin a ride home from the bar. He left his car in the lot after a night out. Stacy didn't drive a sports car, though. I'm not a car girl, but it seemed like a normal vehicle. Nothing that stood out like the one driving away last night.

Q lets out a screech. I realize I'm petting a little too hard. "Sorry, girl," I say. Q gives me a look before demanding to be petted nicely.

If only pets could talk. Q could give me all the answers I need. Who did you see inside our house, leaving a letter for me?

I take out my cell phone and open up the Facebook app. What Amber said about Mary has been on my mind. My husband's ex was a little more than unhinged in the past.

When I search her name on Facebook, a few profiles pop up. I scroll down until I recognize her picture. Mary took a selfie outside on a wooded trail.

She looks so happy. I can see why Kevin was attracted to her. She's gorgeous. She's very active herself. The two likely bonded over their passion for outdoor activities.

Who would have thought their engagement would end with her cheating and acting like a complete lunatic after? The calls to Kev. She scratched my car over a year ago. Right before I found out I was pregnant, she stopped. I was worried she was going to continue to harass us while I was carrying a child. I always wondered if she found out I was pregnant and that's why she stopped.

Did she find out about the miscarriage? I can imagine how happy it would make someone as psycho as her to know I lost a child. The thought of someone finding joy in the worst time of my life makes me sick.

I let out a breath as I click on her Facebook profile. A message pops up on my screen. "You have blocked this person. Do you wish to unblock them?" Below it is a yes or no option. I hesitate before I click yes.

I forgot I blocked her.

Immediately, I'm brought to her profile. She has some restrictions limiting what I can see. Only a few posts on her profile are visible to me. Three pictures pop up on the screen. One is her Facebook profile picture. Underneath it, I can see the several likes and comments she has from her upload. I recognized one of the profiles immediately. Kevin McNeil hearted her profile picture. My stomach feels like it's in knots seeing him like her image. When I look at the date it was posted, I feel relieved seeing that the image was posted three years ago. They were still together at that time, more than likely.

Still, I don't remember the last time Kev liked any of my social media posts or photos.

Mary must not be a big social media user. No new Facebook profile in the past three years?

The second image makes me just as sick. It's one of her and Kevin kissing. Below it is a bunch of heart emojis. Some woman commented, "The big day is coming. Only three more months!"

The big day was supposed to be their wedding. That never happened, of course. Instead, Kev discovered the lies and deceit. He dumped her soon after.

When I scroll down a little, the third picture on her profile literally makes me gasp. Mary is leaning against a car. She's wearing a black tank top and dark sunglasses.

"I have the best fiancé in the world," the caption reads.

My mouth drops as I stare at the picture of the car. It was dark the other night when I saw a car that drove away, but I could swear this is the exact same red sports car.

She's behind this. I let out a nervous laugh. She's doing it again. Mary won't stop until my marriage is burned to the ground just like her engagement was.

Well, I won't let her get away with this.

I open my text message history, scrolling furiously

down. It's frustrating waiting for my phone to load messages from the past two years. For a moment, I worry it's no longer on my cell, after all I didn't just block Mary on Facebook but my phone too.

When I realize I've gone too far, I scroll up and find the text message I sent Mary over a year ago. I read the old message and immediately remember how upset I was when I first sent it.

"If you don't leave me alone, I'll call the cops!"

I smirk at my old message. I didn't allow Mary a chance to reply. I blocked her immediately. I always wondered what she would have said had I given her the opportunity to reply. Well, it's time to find out.

Just like Facebook, when I attempt to send her a message, I get a notification that I need to unblock her. When I do, I immediately type out my message.

"I meant what I said over a year ago, Mary. Leave me and Kevin alone! Or else!"

I hesitate before I hit send. Is this really a smart idea? How unhinged is Mary? You don't mess with crazy people. Yes, I'm upset, but there are limits to how far I'll go. Mary seems like the type to take things to an extreme.

The reason you shouldn't start altercations with people is you never know what the other person is capable of until it's too late to go back. Despite my concerns, my finger hits send. In a moment, the message shows that it was sent.

Too late to go back now.

I continue to text her. "Leave us alone, or there will be consequences." I smirk as I send it. It's my way of telling her I know what she's been doing. I know it's her. I'll use the same language in the letters.

My face drops when I see a check mark beside the

messages. Mary saw them. There's definitely no going back. In the heat of the moment, it felt good sending her the messages but now, at any second, she'll reply. I imagine it won't go well.

Just wait until Kev finds out.

He's so upset with me. What if he doesn't find any of this funny or mature? I stare at my phone, waiting for her reply, hoping I didn't take this too far.

That's when the doorbell rings.

CHAPTER 25

My heart sinks in my chest. She's here. Mary is at my door. I texted her. She saw the message, and instead of replying over the phone, she's at my door.

Don't mess with crazy. Why don't I ever listen to myself when I know I'm doing something stupid?

I don't answer the door. I feel frozen. What if it's not Mary? What if there's another letter?

The third letter I found at work said it warned me to not tell others. What's in store for me when I open that door?

Why open the door at all? Call the police immediately.

The bell rings a second time, making my heart beat faster. This time, whoever's outside isn't going anywhere. They won't run. They won't take off in their car. They won't leave until I answer the door.

"Jo?" a familiar voice calls out. "You home?"

I peek through the side of the curtain and see Trey on the porch. He knocks again.

Relieved, I go towards the front door. Before I open it for him, a voice inside me demands that I stop. "Don't open the door," it says. "You can't trust him."

I hesitate a moment but realize I'm being paranoid. I open the door, and Trey greets me with a smile.

"Hey," he says.

"Hi, Trey," I say. I want to ask him the obvious, but he beats me to it.

"I wanted to check in on you. After that scratch on your car, I'm sure you're a little out of it. Can we talk?"

I nod and gesture for him to come inside. He looks around my house, taking a moment to look at a picture of Kevin and me from our wedding day.

"I spoke with Amber some more after you left," he says. "She told me more about the letter you found." He lets out a sigh. "I didn't realize how intimidating it was. Sorry if I came off cold to you before you left work."

"It's fine, Trey," I say.

"What did Kev say about it?" he asks. "Did you tell him about the car?"

I shake my head. "I'm going to tell him everything today."

That's if he comes home. I don't tell Trey that, though. I don't need to air my dirty laundry much more. I know who's behind this now. My husband's crazy ex-girlfriend is still trying to ruin our marriage.

"Maybe you shouldn't tell him," Trey says. I look at him, surprised.

"What? Why?"

"I thought about it a lot. Whoever it is wants you to find out what Kevin is doing behind your back."

I shake my head. "Trey, I—"

"Hear me out," he says, putting a hand up. "Sure, they're doing it in a weird way, but why would someone go out of their way like this? They want you to know he's cheating. Now, why do they want you to know, that's the part I don't understand."

"He's not cheating," I say, shaking my head.

He makes a face. "Come on, Jo. Amber told me about the text message you found last week on his phone. Now we find out he has a second phone? Why have one?" Before I answer, he puts up another hand. "I know, it's his 'work phone'," he says in a mocking tone. "Come on, Jo," he repeats. "I know it's hard. Don't you see what Kevin's doing to you?"

"What is he doing?"

He shakes his head in disgust. "Ever since he came into the picture, you've been different."

"How?" I say with my own tone. Is Trey somehow hung up on that one date we had ages ago? Does he have feelings for me? Of course he'd be upset that a man like Kevin came into my life if he does.

"You stopped coming out with us to the bar."

I shake my head. "Kevin didn't stop me from coming." Although after I say the words, I question if that's true. Last week, Kevin shamed me for wanting to go out to the bar after work with my coworkers. He mentioned Trey by name as a reason why.

"I'm married now, Trey," I say. "Marriage is work. I put in my time at my cubicle. I also need to put in my time in my marriage."

He stares at me a moment but doesn't say a word. I start to feel uncomfortable. I'm regretting even letting Trey into my house. His usual calm and joyful demeanour changes to one that's rigid.

"He doesn't even know your friends. I've never met him. Amber either. Don't you find that weird…? He's gaslighting you," he says, continuing the attack on my husband.

"Stop, Trey. Just stop. You and I are just friends."

"I know!" he says, raising his voice. "That's why I'm

here. That's why I'm telling you this. He's gaslighting you. He doesn't deserve you. He's cheating on you."

"No, he's not," I say in a calm voice but with a tone that sounds like I'm on the verge of losing it completely. "Now, stop. Kevin's telling me the truth."

"How do you know?" he asks, taking a deep breath, waiting for me to respond.

I open my cell and show him Mary's profile. "See?" I say, showing him the picture of her leaning against the car. "Thats the car I saw last night. It's her. My husband's ex-fiancée is behind this. I know the truth now. She's trying to ruin my marriage—still. Last night, I think she was watching my house from our backyard. I saw this car leaving when I tried to catch her."

Trey blinks at me several times and lowers his head. "But, what—"

I cut him off. "I'm done with this conversation, Trey. I'm not comfortable having you in my home right now. Please leave."

He looks at me in disbelief. I'm waiting for him to continue the argument, but instead he gives in.

"Sorry," he says as he walks past me. "I'm sorry I came." I take a deep breath but don't respond. Instead, I watch as Trey opens the front door and leaves without another word.

When he's outside my house, I quickly lock the door. Taking a deep breath, I look through the peephole at Trey walking slowly down the steps. Before he enters his car that's parked on the street, he turns and looks at my house.

Now I wonder if he knows I'm watching him. He lowers his head as he opens the driver's side door and gets inside.

Why does it feel like I can't trust anyone in my life right now? It's like everyone is against me.

I know who's behind this, though. Mary Halbec. I saw her car last night. Or did I? Maybe nobody was in my backyard. Perhaps it was a sound coming from a neighbor's yard, or the wind pushing the gate open. Even the car could have been entirely coincidental.

There could be many reasons for what I saw. None of them could be what I think.

Is this how it feels like when someone has a mental breakdown? I let out a laugh, wondering if I truly am going insane.

Suddenly, my cell buzzes in my pocket. I take it out. Here we go. Mary has finally replied.

When I unlock my phone, I find out it's not her. It's a photo. I cover my mouth in shock when I read the message below the image.

"You'll never guess what happened to me."

CHAPTER 26

I read the message Amber sent me and look at the image again. Half of her face is badly bruised. An eye is swollen shut.

"What happened?" I text back. But I don't wait for a reply. I call her instead.

Thankfully, she picks up immediately and gives me some relief. "I'm okay," she says. "It looks worse than it is."

"What happened?" I ask again.

"I was attacked."

"What? By who?" I say, confused.

"It all happened so quickly," she says. "Mr. Dunstrow told me that I've been behind on my work lately. I put in some extra hours, hoping to get him off my back today."

I let out a sigh. That's why Amber was at work past her scheduled time. It seems like Mr. Dunstrow is getting on more people's cases than mine.

Amber takes a deep breath over the phone. I can hear the shakiness in her voice. "When I went home, I parked on my street like I always do. When I stepped out, I felt the crushing blow against the side of my face."

"What! Who did it?"

She lets out a nervous laugh. "I don't know. They took my purse. Ugh. I didn't have much money, but all my important documents were inside. Why do I keep my social insurance card in my purse? How stupid can I be? This area is usually pretty safe."

"You didn't see who did this to you?"

"No," she confirms. "I hit the ground hard. I don't think I lost consciousness or anything. It just happened so quickly, and I was just shocked. I know they hit me with a large stone, though. They dropped it when they ran away."

"You didn't look to see who did it to you?"

She lets out a heavy breath. "After a moment, I did. They were wearing a black hoodie. That's all I noticed. That and my purse in their hand as they jetted off."

"I warned you," the letter said today in my car. Now, after I told Amber about the letter, she's assaulted. They took the purse to make it look random.

"I'm so sorry," I say. I cover my mouth in horror.

"It's nobody's fault," she says. "I spoke to the police already. They left just a few moments ago. They were surprised as well. Purse-snatching happens, but not on random streets in the middle of the day. And usually it's not so violent. At least, that's what they tell me."

That's because it wasn't random. Amber was targeted and not for her purse. This is my fault. I know exactly who's behind it too.

"Are you okay?" I ask again.

"I'm okay," she says. "A little shaken up, but okay. This old bag of peas from the back of my freezer is doing wonders." She lets out a nervous laugh. "I guess I wanted to let you know you're not the only one who's a victim of random crimes. Did you report the scratch?"

I let out a sigh of my own. "Not yet."

"I'm going to lay down and relax," she says.

As we end the call, I hate myself for not telling her

the truth. I'm full of rage for what she went through.

I immediately open my text messages with Mary. She's crossed the line now. It's no longer intimidating letters and property damage; she's escalated to violence. Where does this end?

She still hasn't replied to my messages, but I know she's read them. I furiously send another text.

"This isn't funny anymore," I text. "You went too far."

My eyes widen as I see dots at the bottom of the chat. She's not only seen my message, but she's actively writing back now. When her message pops up, I feel rage boiling inside me.

"Go ahead. Call the cops. See what happens if you do," she writes.

CHAPTER 27

I'm not just calling the police; I'm going there in person. With what's happened, I want to show the truth myself. I gather the two letters. The third is in my car.

I'll drive directly to the station. I'm not exactly sure how this works. Do I demand to speak to a detective? Do I have to wait in line and be as patient as possible to speak to an officer?

Should I text Kevin? I sigh when I realize what I'm considering. Am I really about to speak to the police about what's happened but only text my husband? He deserves to know. You can't text your husband that you're leaving to speak to the police because an anonymous stalker attacked your friend.

Mary, you have my attention. She actually thinks I won't report this? My friend is hurt and she thinks I'll stay quiet?

I've been stricken with guilt since seeing Amber's face. Had I reported this anonymous person last week, none of this would have happened.

Or would it have been worse? If Mary is capable of hurting Amber, what else is she capable of?

I take out my cell and call Kevin. I need to leave to go to the police station, but first I need to come clean. I nervously wait for him to answer, but of course he doesn't. Why is it when you absolutely need to reach someone, you can't get a hold of them?

I leave a message for my husband. "Kev, call me right away when you get this." I hang up and start to head to the door.

Q rubs against my hands as I put my shoes on. I don't have time to give her attention right now. I know I need to make one more call. I need to speak to Amber again. I need to come clean. She doesn't know about the second and third letters. She doesn't know because I told her about the letter that I put her in harm's way.

I cringe thinking about how black and blue the side of her face looks. I take out my cell to call her as I open the front door. When I do, a red letter falls onto my feet.

"Read me now."

Again. I look around my house, but of course, I don't see the anybody around. I don't see a red sports car. Nothing.

"Stop!" I scream from my porch. "Leave me alone!"

Whenever I find a new letter from them, my heart beats faster. My pulse goes through the roof. I'm absolutely petrified.

Not this time, though. I'm sure I'm visibly steaming. How dare Mary do this to me?

I pick up the letter and open it, hating myself for doing exactly what she wants me to do. My anger turns to confusion as I read what's inside.

"He's on a date with a woman at the restaurant Amore. Hurry."

CHAPTER 28

I called Amber. We met at the police station parking lot. I showed her the letters. She understands that she was targeted by the person writing the letters. I spoke with detectives.

These are all the things I wish I did in the fictional world where things I do make sense.

Instead, I hightail it to the restaurant. The letter said I needed to hurry. My husband is on an actual date with a woman. I imagine going there and seeing him with Stacy Wingham.

"It's just a work dinner."

I can already imagine what Kev would say if I saw them together. I can almost imagine them feeding each other appetizers or sharing a single strand of spaghetti like a cheesy romcom.

I never drove to a destination so quickly. Amore is an Italian restaurant about twenty minutes from my house, but I managed to cut that time to fourteen minutes by being a little creative with my driving. Yellow means drive faster and only sometimes red means slow down.

There was something about this letter that compelled me to listen. I felt the urge to come to the restaurant to find out if it's true. The fact that the anonymous person wrote the word "hurry" was also different.

Maybe Trey was right. Whoever's doing this wants me to find out the truth. They also want to stay anonymous.

Amber was viciously attacked by whoever's doing this.

When Mary texted me back, telling me to see what happens if I contact the police, it nearly confirmed their identity. Despite that, I can't stop second guessing myself and everyone around me.

Also, I hate that the restaurant is Amore. It had to be that one. The lighting is perfect inside. With the dim lights and flickering candles on the beige tablecloth, it sets the perfect romantic mood. This restaurant was where Kevin told me he loved me for the first time. I was so enthralled that I spilt my wine on the table. I was so embarrassed but happy at the same time. Now he's bringing another woman there? The thought of it makes my stomach turn.

I see the restaurant ahead as I drive towards it. Typically, in downtown Calgary, it's pretty difficult to find an empty spot on a road you don't have to pay for. Today's my lucky day, though. There's an empty spot right in front of the restaurant.

However, that may make it a little more difficult to do what I plan. I feel stupid for plotting out this idea. It's summer and boiling hot, but I put on a loose black hoodie from home before I left. Sure, I may stick out in a fancy Italian restaurant if I go inside dressed the way I am, but I need some way to prevent Kevin from easily spotting me.

That's if he's even there.

I had all this time to reverse what I planned when I

read the fourth letter. Instead of doing what's logical and going to the police, I'm here. Sneaking about where my husband may be to find out if he's being faithful. How many times will I do this to myself? What will I need to confirm that my husband is not doing anything wrong? That he's not hiding anything?

My face drops when I spot his car across the street in front of the restaurant. So much for that thought. Seems like I'm not the only lucky one when it comes to finding parking spots.

That's not all. He's walking along the sidewalk towards the restaurant. And, just as the letter suggested, he's not alone. Slightly ahead of him is a woman in a slender white dress.

Their backs are to me as they head toward the restaurant.

I turn my wheel and park in a no-parking zone, watching them closely. All it would take is for him to turn his head slightly and my cover would be broken.

Thankfully, he doesn't. They go to the front door of the restaurant. She smiles at him and enters. That's when I see her face.

I expected to see him with Stacy. I figured it would be her that he would be with. Had I caught him with his coworker, I would have gotten the same old excuse as before. "We're just out for a work dinner. What's wrong with you?"

I let out a sigh. I was right. There is someone, only it isn't anyone I know.

This woman is notably younger than Kevin. From a distance, I put her in her mid-twenties. Isn't it all so cliche? An older man having an affair with a young pretty woman.

Kev wanted something new. Something shiny and young. He doesn't want his boring wife who eats too much junk food while watching reality television.

Affairs felt like a concept that happened on TV or movies. Never would I think in a million years I'd be following my husband around to find out who's he's sleeping with behind my back.

The woman has orangish hair and completes the Irish look with freckles that I could spot from my car. She's gorgeous.

That makes me think of Mary Halbec. If she's truly behind this, I suppose I owe her a big thank you. I remind myself what happened to Amber. Nobody deserves that, though.

I catch my thoughts and remind myself that I haven't really seen much. I saw my husband and a woman I don't know walk into a restaurant. That's it. I didn't see them come from his car. I didn't see them embrace. I didn't see them kiss.

He opened a door for her and stepped inside.

I remind myself that Kevin wants a break. Is that what this means? A break for him is him running to the arms of a pretty redhead?

But in marriage, there's no such thing as breaks. The power of the ring is supposed to mean you don't just walk away so easily. And yet, here I am.

I drive past, slowly. Thankfully for me, Kev picked the best restaurant for me to discover him having an affair in. Amore has a row of windows that allow me to peek inside.

I drive around, attempting to find parking that's not too close to the restaurant, and end up driving a solid few minutes before I find a space. I take a deep breath before stepping outside my car.

Now what?

I know what my plan is. Well, sort of. I need to see them. I need to see them embrace. I need to see them kiss. I need to watch them flirt. As terrible as that all sounds, I need definitive proof that he's cheating.

I can't keep living this way. I'm going insane trying to figure out who's lying and who's telling the truth.

Never would I have thought I'd end up this way. I trusted my husband. I love my husband. But now I'm trusting the words of an anonymous letter over the man I love.

Even before the letters started, I suspected something was up. More and more, he's spent less time with me. More and more, I suspected he was spending that time with someone else who has his heart. I thought it was coming from my own insecurities. I thought it was from the trauma of what we lost.

But the letters are telling me differently.

I walk down the block towards the restaurant. I'm not a fan of walking around downtown. I'm always so hypervigilant by myself. But those concerns are furthest from my mind right now.

All I can think about is the smile Kevin brandished as he opened the door for the young woman.

No wonder he didn't want to come home tonight. He had a hot date planned. Why go home to the old ball and chain when you have her replacement ready?

How could Mary know about him having a date tonight, though? It's another reason I continue to question if she's truly behind this. How could his ex-fiancée know what he was intending to do tonight?

I think of Stacy Wingham. Maybe he talked about

what he was planning to do at work with her. That could be how Stacy would know.

I can almost hear Trey's words in my mind. The writer of the letters wants me to know the truth. Why, though? That's the real question. Why would someone go out of their way to show a wife that her husband is cheating on them? Why would someone be so invested in this?

I look down the block and Amore is now in sight. Here we go.

What are the chances that I'll see Kevin and his special dinner date if I just walk by the restaurant? Thankfully, my husband chose a restaurant with enough exterior windows for me to try and find out what he may be doing.

I let out a sigh.

When I catch them, it will change everything. There's no going back once you know the truth. Once that trust is broken, you'll never regain it.

That makes me think of why Kevin is so upset with me. He knows my trust is wavering. With the fourth letter and me knowing he's inside that restaurant with another woman, it's too late.

The fast-paced walk to the restaurant is starting to take its toll. I can feel how sweaty I am under the heavy hoodie I'm wearing. I feel like I'm being baked inside my clothing. I pull my hood over my head and open the camera app on my cell.

It's not the most intricate plan, but then again, I didn't have enough time to prepare. I feel like I've had no time to think about what I'm doing either. I'm purely reacting to everything that's happening.

I take a deep breath as I near the front of the

restaurant and hit record on my camera. This is it. I'll walk by and try to catch them on video. I'm not sure what I'll do if I don't see them, but this is a solid start to my plan.

I imagine catching him kissing the freckled girl on the lips as I walk by. I'm not sure what I'll be more upset by. Part of me wants to catch him in the act just to know that I'm not going insane.

I take my first step by the restaurant window and hold my camera awkwardly up as I walk, pretending to look on my phone while aiming it inside the restaurant.

That's when I see him. Kevin's sitting at a table at the edge of the restaurant. He's at the first table I see. Only he's sitting alone and looking outside the window.

And he's looking directly at me.

CHAPTER 29

I never thought I was capable of running so fast. In fact, I don't remember the last time I had to run.

I had my cell perfectly positioned to catch a video of Kevin with his date. Instead, I saw him sitting alone at a table. Nobody with him. The freckled redhead was nowhere to be found.

And, worst of all, Kevin saw me, I think. He was literally looking directly at me.

But I didn't stick around to confirm. I turned my head and ran in the other direction. Maybe I got lucky. After all, I had my black hoodie on. It covered most of my face as I walked by the window, at least I thought so. He wasn't expecting me. I could have easily been a jogger, just innocently running by. A jogger wearing a thick sweater in eighty-degree weather. And it's not at all odd that this random jogger bolted the opposite direction suddenly.

And I still haven't stopped. I'm scared that if I do, I'll turn and see Kevin behind me. How would I even explain this?

Of course, my grand plan of catching my husband having an affair ends with him discovering me. I'm not so good at this sneaking around stuff.

My heart pounds as I make it several blocks away

from the restaurant. I pause, leaning against the brick exterior of a corner store. When I look around, I don't recognize where I am.

I'm lost on top of it all. Out of breath, I try to calm my nerves to think clearly.

I take out my cell, half expecting Kevin to have texted me, "Hey, was that you?" or, "Hey, WTF?"

Thankfully, there's no message. As I catch my breath, I realize I'm a few blocks away from my car. Now I'm glad I didn't park near the restaurant. Kev could have easily seen me.

There is the odd chance that he didn't recognize me. As stupid as the thought is, I hope that's the case. How could he not recognize his own wife, though?

I cross the street, turning at another intersection. When I see my car, I let out a nervous smile. I pat my workout pants and panic when I don't feel my keys.

Of course.

Did they fall out during my escape? Are they somewhere in the gutters of downtown Calgary? Perfect. I put my hand inside the front pocket of my hoodie and let out another nervous laugh. I found my keys.

I may have lost my sanity though.

This is ridiculous. Every time I receive a letter, I put myself in a position where I look foolish. How many times will I continue to do this until I realize that whoever is sending me the letters is not exactly my friend?

They're not my enemy either, though.

Kevin was at the restaurant with a woman. Although, I don't know why she wasn't sitting with him once inside. Maybe she went to the restroom.

Or maybe she wasn't with him.

My thoughts run wild as I open my car door. I sit in

the driver's seat and slam the door shut. Defeated, I lean my head against the steering wheel. I could slam my head into the horn out of frustration.

It's as if the letters I receive are all half-truths. Or I'm just not lucky enough to discover the truth.

Is my husband having an affair? Is the person sending the letters trying to help me discover the truth? Or is this all one big game, and I'm the main contestant. And what's the prize?

A divorce.

That's the end result. No matter what, that's how the show ends. Either I find out he's been cheating and leave him. Or he discovers what I've been up to and leaves me.

The worse part is, I can't stop playing this terrible game. I need to know the truth. I need to know who's sending me these letters. I need to know what Kevin is doing, if anything at all.

I can't stop now. Part of me knows the right thing to do is come clean. Tell Amber the truth about why she was attacked. Tell Kevin about the letters. Report it all to the police.

Instead, I know I won't do that. I can't. If I do, I won't be able to find out what the anonymous person knows.

My phone buzzes. On the screen I see his name and know the end of the game may be coming sooner than I thought. My eyes widen as I read a new message from Kevin.

CHAPTER 30

When I arrive back home, I slump on the couch. Q immediately jumps on my lap, purring. She paws at my shoulder, demanding attention.

I give it to her, petting her. I feel a tear welling in my eye as I do. Everything is coming to an end. The message from Kevin only proves it.

"I'm not coming home tonight," he texted. "I'll be staying at a hotel."

I texted him if we could talk. His reply though didn't make me feel any better. "Not tonight."

When I asked him what hotel he was staying at, he didn't reply. He read my message. A green check mark was under my text, but he didn't respond.

Why can't he tell me where he's staying? Is it because he's taking the pretty redhead back to his room?

"I had fun last night. Let's do that again sometime." The text message from last week haunts me. I'm sure they'll be having fun tonight.

This is how my marriage ends. Never go to sleep angry. Well, what do you do when your husband refuses to even sleep in the same bed?

There was a time I thought I knew who my husband was. Nothing he's been doing makes sense. Him staying at a hotel room overnight makes no sense. Did he bring any clothes with him? Did he bring a bar of soap with him?

Kevin hates the small bars of soap hotels provide. Whenever we go on a trip, he brings his own. I thought it was funny seeing a man pack soap with him on our honeymoon. I thought it was cute.

He thinks ahead. He plans things out, unlike me. My behaviour has shown that lately. What was I thinking today? Sneaking around in a hoodie trying to snap photos of my husband and his date inside a restaurant. Did I really think I could get away with something like that?

The adrenaline in the moment made me think I could. As scared as I was to see what Kevin was up to with the woman, part of me thought I was being slick.

I imagined taking a picture of the two of them at dinner. I'd print it. Blow it up to a poster size. When Kevin came home, I'd show him the lovely new artwork in the house. I'd leave him, telling him what a terrible person he was for gaslighting me. Making me believe I was the one going crazy when he was one two-timing me.

That's far from what happened. Instead, I was caught. My hand was fully engulfed in the cookie jar. I still can't believe it. He was just sitting at the first table I saw, by himself, looking right at me. What are the chances of that?

I considered asking him if he saw me. I could text and see what he says. I imagine what his response would be if he didn't see me and I admit to what I did.

Ms. Q snuggles her petite face against mine. I smile as she digs her head against my chin, licking me several times. Her tongue's worse than sandpaper but it makes me laugh.

I rub her fur and kiss the top of her furry head. I almost want to thank her for breaking me out of my spell. Only, my terrible thoughts rush back to me nearly immediately when I think of my precious Q.

What happens to her if Kevin and I divorce? Everyone talks about custody of children following a separation. I have no clue how it works with pets. I picked Q from the pet store. Kevin didn't even want her. I was the one who fell in love with her that day. Kevin wasn't fond of the idea of having a pet at all. He tried to talk me out of getting her entirely.

"How about a goldfish?" he actually suggested before going inside the pet store.

I suppose that means I'd have Q to myself. But Kevin's grown to love her too. Do we have a weird post-divorce custody of a cat? Do we switch weekly with her? Would he pay me for cat support?

Somehow the humor helps me not to think about how terrible my life will be if we divorce. Kevin's aged wonderfully. He's lost weight since we first met.

I'm a complete mess. I'm heading towards diabetes. I've nearly all but given up on taking care of myself.

Q nudges her head against my chin again, as if to tell me that everything will be okay. But I don't think it will be.

I feel a tear welling in my eye again as I think about it. Sure, since Kevin makes more than me, I'd likely have alimony. The only asset we share is the house, but he bought it before we started dating.

I kiss Q on the head again. Her face wrinkles as I do.

I put my hand in front of her, and she licks it. "I don't care what happens," I say out loud to my cat, "you're coming with me."

The idea of divorce makes me physically ill. I take out my cell. Kevin still hasn't replied.

Defeated and knowing that my life has completely burnt to the ground, I open a text message. My sadness turns to anger as I type out the words.

"If you know what's going on, just tell me!" I text Mary. "No more games, please! Just tell me. I need to know."

Almost immediately, Mary reads my message. I stare at my screen, anticipating her reply. No more letters. No more intimidation. You have my full attention. My life is already ruined. Just tell me what's happening.

She doesn't reply, though. She doesn't say a word.

CHAPTER 31

I sit in my cubicle, hating myself even more than I did the day before. Kev hasn't texted or called. I don't know where my husband is, or who he's with.

At this point, I almost wish I'd get another ominous letter that spells out everything. I don't care anymore. I just need to know the truth. The actual truth. No games. I don't know who's gaslighting me more, Kevin or the letters.

Mary hasn't responded to my text. It was so difficult to sleep last night. It was hard to fall asleep, and when I did, I'd wake up throughout the night, looking at my phone for a reply from either Kevin or Mary. Neither did.

Now I'm at work. Another beautiful day at my job. I've already had several terrible calls today. I managed to get through them. I even managed to smile at Mr. Dunstrow when he popped by my cubicle to see what I was up to. It feels like I have several stalkers.

Wouldn't it be amusing if it was Mr. Dunstrow who was behind it all? The man seems to have a mission in life to be utterly annoying.

I was in the middle of a terrible call when Mr. Dunstrow entered my cubicle. As the customer was giving me crap for the rise in his energy costs, Mr. Dunstrow smiled at me and gave me a thumbs up.

I smiled back and gave him one finger back. My thumb. I wish it was another finger though. I hate this job. I hate my life. I hate whoever is sending me these letters. I hate myself most of all for letting myself get to this point.

Amber isn't at work today. Makes sense to take a day off after being viciously assaulted. Amber puts on a smile for others, but I know that must have been scary. If I was assaulted getting out of my car, I'd never leave my house again. I'd need years of therapy. Well, after what's happened to me, we both need it.

I just want to know the truth. Is that so difficult to figure out? Why is it so hard? I deserve to know what's happening. I deserve to know why it's happening.

I'm being targeted. The scratched car, the harassing and intimidating letters, and now Amber. I always knew that Mary was a little off. Her behaviour in the past was so crazy.

What if it's not her, though?

I can't just sit in my cubicle and take more terrible phone calls from terrible people and wait for another anonymous letter. I can't handle any more lies or revelations that my husband is keeping from me. But how can I discover the truth?

I look at my computer screen and smile when I have an idea. It's time I start being active in discovering what's really happening. I'm not a complete victim. I can do something to figure this out.

I'll march right up to Mary and find out for myself what she's doing. I'll knock on her door, show her the letters and demand that she tells the truth. She can call the cops. Perfect. I'll show them pictures of what Mary did to Amber. That's how to fast-track discovering the truth.

I've heard that you don't get far with making a scene. You can win more people over with honey than vinegar.

That's not true though.

If working at Nexen Power has helped me realize anything, it's the more you complain, sometimes the better treatment you get. I can't tell you the number of people who call and complain on a monthly basis. How do we treat them? A lot of times, we give them something. An extra perk. Something for us to say: we provided good customer service. Sure, it's at the risk of the employees' sanity though. I'm not allowed to give them away. Only supervisors are.

If the cops are forced to come to Mary's house, the truth will be discovered. I just have one problem. I don't know where Mary lives.

Today may be the only time I ever felt happy to work at an electric company. Unless you're Amish, we have a product everybody needs. And there's limited competition. If you own or rent a house in the city and its vicinity, chances are, you used our company before.

Now, this is something you are definitely not supposed to do. I open a search and type in Mary's full name. After I do, several addresses pop up in our system. Seems like she has had a few accounts with us. The most recent address is at the top of the screen.

I smile when I see the account is still active. This is her current address.

Knowing what I'm doing is wrong, I look behind me. If Mr. Dunstrow found out I was using our system to confirm the address of my husband's ex-fiancée, I'd fast track my firing to today. Thankfully, nobody is there.

I take out a notepad and jot down her address. It's in

the south of the city, further out from the city limits but still considered part of Calgary's electric grid.

I see an X beside her name and click on it. Another reason we're not supposed to look up people we know on our system is we can see who's having financial difficulty.

Mary's behind on her bills by nearly a thousand dollars. Her account is not just in bad standing but close to getting her utilities cut entirely.

Those are the worst calls. I imagine being the one having to call Mary to discuss her account issues. Looking through her account, I see we've tried calling a few times already. So many people ignore us until they find themselves completely in the dark. That's when the real nasty calls come.

Seriously, I hate this job.

Satisfied that I got her address, I smile. Now it's time for me to find the courage to spew a little lie. The workday is more than half done, but I can't sit in this cubicle any longer. I need to leave. I need to find out what's happening. It's time for me to stop letting all these terrible things happen to me and do something about it.

What if it's not her, though? I feel myself doubting everything and everyone around me. There's a chance it may not be Mary Halbec.

I open a new search and start typing out another name.

This is so bad. I never thought I'd use my work like this. When I help teach trainees when they start working here, there's a half-day course on ethics. Once I even taught it. It was actually Amber's training class. Part of that class is telling new trainees to never use our system to look up people we know in our personal lives. Accounts have a lot of personal information.

So much for ethics, I guess.

When I finish typing out Stacy Wingham, I wait impatiently for results to show. Stacy only has one account with us. It's active and in good standing. I jot down her address and can feel my conscience telling me what I'm doing is wrong.

A knock on my partial cubicle wall scares me. I turn and see Trey with a coffee in one hand and a cribbage board with a deck of cards in his other. He smiles wide at me.

"Hey," he says.

I quickly turn and power off my monitor. "Uh, hey," I say, stumbling over myself. When I turn back to him, he looks at me oddly. "What's up?" I ask.

He lets out a sigh. "Listen, the other day, I overstepped. I'm sorry. This is my peace offering." He hands out a coffee to me, and I graciously take it. I feel like a zombie with the few hours of broken sleep I managed last night. "Mocha with extra whipped cream. Plus, I'll let you skunk me today in cribbage." He lets out a laugh.

He stares at me, his grin widening. There's something about the way he's looking at me that makes me feel unsettled. "I don't like how you talked about my marriage yesterday," I say.

He nods and purses his lips. "Yeah, I'm sorry. I was trying to be a friend. I'm worried about you."

"I can handle myself," I say.

He looks at me and glances away. "I don't know what's happening with you and Kevin. I know you have Amber to talk to about this too, I know I made a scene the other night, but I'm just going to say this: you look super stressed out. I won't bother you for details, though. If you need someone to talk to, just know that I'm here, okay?"

I nod. "Okay. Thanks. Sorry if I came off a little too strong the other night as well."

He gives me a thin smile. "That was completely on me. I need to realize that not everybody needs to know my opinion." He puts the cribbage game on my desk. "So, what about a quick game? We can even play muggins too."

He grins at me again, and as he does, I can't help but feel my stomach turn. I'm not sure if it's paranoia or if I'm justified. Sometimes it feels like I can't trust anybody in my life.

"I have to go," I say, standing up from my chair. "Thanks for the mocha." I grab the cup and my purse, brushing past Trey.

"Where are you going?" he asks.

"I don't feel well."

CHAPTER 32

My husband still hasn't returned home. He went out on a date and stayed in a hotel room last night.

My life has completely spiraled out of control, and I have no clue what's happening. But I know someone who knows the truth.

I stare outside my car window at Mary's house, tucked away on a quiet stretch of a rural country road. Large farm fields stretch out on either side of the small property. I know from our system that she's renting the house.

It's not the address I imagined a woman like Mary would be living in. I know it's her, though. While I'm not completely sure how old my husband's ex-fiancée is, the birthday of a Mary Halbec on our system with this address is about what I assume her to be.

Already I'm a little uneasy. If Mary is the one leaving me letters, will confronting her be a good idea? Look what happened to Amber. Would she hesitate to do the same to me? Likely not. But I'm not defenseless.

Kevin is a very active man. He likes being outside. He enjoys biking, hunting, hiking, skiing, off grid camping, and many more activities I find horrendous. We are complete opposites in that way.

His love for the outdoors is part of the reason he

loved our one-year anniversary at the cabin he rented.

Every summer, knowing that Kevin will want to do something that involves me being outdoors, I prepare myself. I buy bear spray. We live in one of the few areas in the world where you could be walking around and stumble upon a grizzly. So of course I buy bear spray regularly.

Kev makes fun of me for it, but I'd rather be prepared than... mauled.

This year, with how busy Kevin's been at work, I didn't buy a new can. The one I have has been expired for several months. Hopefully that doesn't mean it won't be effective.

I wouldn't be using it on a grizzly, though. I'm sure even if it lost some potency from being expired, the bear spray would still work on a crazy ex-girlfriend.

Slipping the can into my purse, I look at the rearview mirror and pray I won't have to use it. I'm not a violent person. I've never been in a fight. I'm not looking for trouble.

All I want is to peacefully knock on her door, find out the truth, and leave with no fuss. I look in the rearview mirror again. Am I really going to be so naive as to believe this won't escalate? Do I really believe this won't go bad?

I open my text messages from Mary and reread them. All of our texts have been so confrontational and aggressive. We both wanted the same thing, Kevin, only I was the winner. Although, my prize may leave me permanently, and it's all because of Mary.

I could still leave. I don't have to knock on her door. I don't have to do anything.

I'd be annoyed with myself if I let this continue

much longer. The letters have made me insane. What Mary is doing to me is far from fair or appropriate. It's illegal.

It needs to stop. But before it does, I also need the truth.

Look at how much trouble I went through to get Mary's address. I can't leave. I broke my company's rules by searching for her. I went to Mr. Dunstrow and told him I wasn't feeling well. I said I had to take the rest of the day off. He wasn't impressed. He asked me to try and "trooper it out", as he called it, but I explained that I needed to leave.

That was certainly not a lie.

Now I'm here, outside Mary's house, about to make another mistake. But the car wreck I call my everyday life must go on. I'm committed now.

I open my door and step out, letting out a deep breath. I look around the small property. Her sports car isn't in the small driveway, but there's the attached garage that it could be parked in. Kevin told me some time ago that Mary was a nurse who worked midnights. Likely she's home and fast asleep inside.

I reluctantly take a few steps towards her porch, my mind racing as I look at the front door. To the side are several rolled up newspapers that appear to have been haphazardly tossed on her porch. As my brain tells me how stupid I am for even attempting this, I unzip my purse, knowing the protection I have is there if I need it.

Although, the fact that I can feel a strong breeze on my face has me worried. Using the bear spray would likely impact me just as much as her if I needed to use it.

Despite my concerns and the voice inside me shouting to go back to my car, I knock on the door.

Knowing she works midnights, I figure it will take some time for her to get up from her bed. I wait patiently for her. After what feels like forever, I knock again.

Nothing. I don't hear anything coming from inside. I start pounding on the front door. I don't care how tired she is, we need to talk.

After another few moments and realizing this isn't going how I planned, I step back. I peer through the window next to the front door but it's difficult to make out anything with the drapes mostly closed. All I have for visibility inside her house is a sliver the closed drapes don't hide.

That small window of vision doesn't give many signs of life. A red couch pillow is on the floor. I notice a TV stand near it. It is the only thing that gives me hope. A bottle of beer is on the stand. Even better, it's a half-drunk bottle.

Someone's home. It's past two. I imagine Mary unwound with a beer after a long shift. Or maybe she woke up not too long ago and had her alcoholic beverage.

Kevin mentioned she likes to drink as well. A woman who likes fast cars, drinks beer and loves being active. On paper, she was perfect for Kevin.

Seeing no movement inside, I realize she won't be coming to the door if she is home. Maybe she doesn't work midnights anymore. She could be at work right now, or maybe she's not a nurse now. The letters I've been receiving don't seem to be coming from someone who's in a good place in life. I imagine that Mary isn't doing so well.

She could be inside and just refusing to open the door. "Mary!" I shout out, walking back to the door. I knock hard. "We need to talk. It's Josie."

I'm suddenly thankful that she lives in the middle of nowhere so nobody can see how crazy I look. If anybody went through what I've been through, they would be within their rights to be a little more than upset. Mary is lucky I don't attempt to break in her door or window. Movies make it look so easy to do.

I think of the scratch on my car. She's lucky she didn't park her fancy sports car in the driveway.

"Mary," I say again and peer inside her house. I look for any clue that she could be home. A moving shadow inside, changes in the lighting, anything.

Frustrated, I take out my cell and text her. "We need to talk. I'm outside your house right now. I just want the truth."

Just like before, a green check appears almost immediately. Mary saw my text. She's not replying, though. I peer inside her window again but don't see any movement.

Why isn't she saying something? If a woman showed up at my front door and started knocking furiously, peering inside my house and texting me, I'd have some sort of reaction.

I'd call the police at a minimum.

It hits me that this must be her plan. Get me to look like the bad guy in the situation. She could go to Kevin, police report in hand, and show him how crazy I've been. Well, I have the letters I could show him. Wasn't the police showing up part of my plan anyway?

Completely defeated, my adrenaline starts to wind down, and I realize how insane I must appear. I slowly head down the porch steps, hoping as I do the door behind me will open.

It doesn't.

She's not here, and if she is, she won't be answering the door. I let out a heavy breath, feeling worse and with more questions than I did when I arrived. I lower my head and look back. The rolled-up collection of newspapers near the front door makes me think of the cut-up letters in the special cards I've been receiving.

CHAPTER 33

I may feel like a complete psycho stalker, but that doesn't stop me from what I do next. I wrote down two addresses before leaving work today. Now, I sit outside Stacy Wingham's house.

It's exactly the type of house I pictured perfect Stacy Wingham living in. Everything is prim and proper. The lawn outside is maintained perfectly. She has an abundance of different types of flowers in a small garden. Long pink peonies stick up above the rest.

I love peonies. I've tried to grow them several times but Calgary's climate works against me. Not for Stacy, though.

I already knocked on her door, but she didn't answer. This time I won't leave until I speak to her.

For a moment, I was nervous that Stacy may have roommates or something. The house is not large and truly perfect for a single woman. You can obviously tell that Stacy takes pride not just in her appearance but her home as well.

I wasn't totally surprised that she wasn't home. Kevin never comes back to our house around this time. Usually, it's well past six in the evening before I see him. Why would I expect that his colleague would be back home sooner than him?

I sigh when I think of Kevin and our house. Will I ever see him return? Will he divorce me without coming back?

The thought of it angers me more. I wish Stacy was here right now. I'd scream at her for what she's done.

I can't get out of my head that I may be wrong about Mary being the person behind the letters. The only other logical person it could be is Stacy.

I could be wrong about both of these women, though. Maybe it's a blessing that Stacy isn't home for me to accuse her of something she hasn't done.

But what has she done with my husband? The letter said Kevin's a cheater. She came to my house with Kevin as well when they didn't expect me there.

It's all so very frustrating. And Stacy could be behind it all.

I thought I was going to be super bored as I sat near Stacy's house waiting for her to return. You watch television shows and see FBI agents in a van listening to wire taps or waiting to spot the bad guy. They don't seem bored. Boxes of pizza, stale donuts and cold coffee surround them. I didn't plan this out too well. Right after I was done at Mary's house, I came directly here. I'm still wearing my black hoodie, which I left in my car from the other day. It has a smell to it, likely from my sprint from Amore.

That doesn't set me off, though. Instead, I'm in the zone. No useless carbs needed to stay focused. I'm able to listen to some music at a very low level and watch Stacy's house without issues.

After the first hour, I assumed my energy level would drain to nothing and I'd bore myself to sleep, but I'm still as hypervigilant as I was when I first arrived. I have one goal. Figure out what's happening in my life. Discover the truth no matter what it takes. I tried to confront Mary, and since that failed, I'm on to my next suspect on the shortlist of who's ruining my life.

I can't help but smile when I see a familiar car come up the road. Slouching in my seat, I peer through the windshield. Stacy's garage door opens slowly, and she pulls in. She doesn't close the garage door behind her.

This is what I was waiting for. This is what I patiently stared outside my windshield for nearly two hours for, but now that she's here, I feel paralyzed. Frozen.

This could go very bad. I want to confront her but don't know what to say. In my imagination, I picture just yelling at her for what she put me through. I didn't really put too much effort into how to start that conversation.

She'd be confused as to how I ended up at her doorstep as well. How do I even explain that without causing a whirlwind of trouble?

I glance at the passenger seat beside me where I have several of the anonymous letters. I look over them. "Read me now," they all demand. I did. Each and every time, I did exactly what the letters asked of me. Each and every time, I failed to learn anything and only embarrassed myself more.

What if I put Stacy in the same position she put me in? I could stack the letters in front of her door. I could see her reaction from my car as she reads the letters, knowing that I know it's her, and that I know where she lives.

I'll even ring the doorbell like what happened with the first letter. Although I imagine I wouldn't be able to make it back to my car by the time she opens her door.

Good. If she sees me, I'll show her the rest of the letters. I'll show her why I've been going crazy with jealousy.

"Crazy". Isn't that what she called me when I found her and my husband at our house alone, drinking. No, wait, *working*. Isn't that the excuse Kevin used?

After seeing him with that woman in the restaurant, it feels like Trey was right. Kevin's been gaslighting me about what he's been up to.

My only question now is how many women were there? Stacy Wingham. Mary Halbec. That redhead from the restaurant last night. How many more? How many lies has he told me? How stupid was I to trust my husband?

Feeling my rage boil inside me, I grab one of the heart-shaped letters beside me and exit my car. I storm up the block towards Stacy's house. I'll ring the doorbell. I'll wait for pretty and perky Stacy to open the door and shove the letter in her face. No need to run. I made sure I grabbed the letter that talked about her being at my house. Even if she's not the one leaving me the letters, she'll have some explaining to do.

Breaking me from my rage-filled fantasy, I notice her car start up inside the garage. Within moments, she's backing out. My eyes widen and I feel my heart pound.

It's almost as if she knew I was coming. In the moment, I panic and put my hoodie over my head, turning around and walking the opposite way.

Why is it every time I try to be sneaky, the person I'm following sees me point blank? This isn't like yesterday, though. I don't think she saw me.

If she exits onto the street and comes my way there's a chance she could spot me.

Maybe I am the crazy woman she thinks I am.

I take a deep breath and consider running. My car is

only half a block away. Where would I go? I keep walking and pray she doesn't see me. I have a fifty-fifty chance she'll head the opposite way.

I'm not lucky. I never am.

Sure enough, she drives slowly past me. I look from the corner of my eye, my hoodie hiding most of my face.

I imagine her rolling down her window and calling out my name.

I guess my luck is better than I thought. She doesn't stop. She drives past me and begins picking up speed down the street.

Where is she going? She just got home. Why is she already leaving?

I never got a text or call from Kevin all day. Are him and Stacy meeting up somewhere? Are they going out for drinks again? Or maybe they're going to be doing more "work" out of his hotel room.

I need to find out for myself. I run to my car and start the ignition. I turn my wheel frantically and enter the street much faster, heading towards her. I need to catch up, but my eyes widen when I see a children playing sign, demanding that I slow down.

What am I doing? I slow down and ask myself the same question out loud. How much of my sanity have I already lost because of what's happened and how much more am I willing to lose?

The question answers itself when I spot Stacy's car in the distance. I push down the pedal and drive faster to catch up. The image of her in my husband's arms keeps me from moving forward. The sound of her laughter in my house the night I caught them in my living room keeps me from turning around and going home.

I need to know where she's going.

This is my first time tailing someone. I have to say, I'm doing well. I keep a four-car distance away from her. I've watched enough detective shows to know you don't follow too closely. Rookie mistake.

I should have been a private detective.

To my surprise, she turns into a parking lot with one large store. Sam's Hobby and Craft Store.

A craft store?

Of course. That makes sense. Seems like my anonymous letter writer needs more supplies. Stacy Wingham likes to take her time to present herself well to the world. She's not lazy with anything she does. She takes pride in her appearance and her house. Of course she takes her time with the letters she's been sending me, coming to a store like this to get the materials she needs.

That makes me think of the rolled-up newspapers at Mary's house. A large supply of letters to cut out and make her ominous warnings to me.

I wish I knew for sure who's doing this.

Stacy enters the store as I slowly step out of my car. I must admit that I'm surprised that she came here. I expected to see her go directly to my husband.

This may be even better, though. I open my cell and start a recording. If I catch her getting the supplies she needs to make the letters I'm receiving, that will be all the proof I need.

I enter the store with my hoodie on. I spot myself on a CCTV camera that's recording the entrance and has a camera showing me in the recording hung on the ceiling. "Thieves will be prosecuted" a sign says on the monitor. I stand out like a sore thumb. In the middle of the summer, I'm wearing a full sweater. It wouldn't take much for Stacy to see me. I need to be careful.

I walk by a few aisles until I see Stacy halfway down one of them. I glance at her. She doesn't notice me. She's entirely entranced by whatever she's looking for. Around her are different paints and colored card. I'm not a crafty person, but it looks like it could be the same type of cardboard the handmade letters are made from.

I walk past the aisle, into the next, hiding myself. I pretend to look at the products on the shelf, trying to figure out what to do. I didn't get a good shot of Stacy with my recording. I'll wait until she's going to the cashier with everything. It will be easier to see what she has purchased and harder for her to refute being the anonymous letter writer when I see what she's buying.

I take a deep breath, wondering how long I have to wait. A crochet pink bunny smiles back at me on the shelf. I look around at the small, knitted animals. I'm a fan of crafts but never found myself trying to do one.

I hear it's good for anxiety to color. I smirk at the idea of buying an adult coloring book after I'm done following Stacy around. Maybe if I purchase one, I can stop being a complete mess.

My thoughts are broken when I see Stacy walking into the aisle I'm in. I turn my head immediately and look at the pink bunny as if asking it to help me not get caught. I glance at Stacy getting closer and know I need to get out of here. I turn to make my escape.

"Josie?" I hear her soft voice and know my cover is broken. Perfect.

I'm really not good at this.

I imagine what would happen if I frantically ran away like I did when Kevin spotted me. Somehow, I imagine it won't work out as well.

I pull off my hoodie and look at Stacy, managing to

put on the best acting performance I can manage. "Stacy? What are you doing here?"

She lets out a laugh. "Just buying some craft stuff." She looks at the pink bunny in front of me. "I didn't know you were a crochet girly." She smiles. "I have that bunny at home."

I look back at the pink bunny in disgust but hide my true expression as I smile back at her. "I'm not really good at it. Trying something new."

"Well, that's a good one to start with," she says with an oddly cheerful tone. "Good for beginners." Just from her playful voice, I know she's messing with me.

She saw me when I came inside the store. She saw me as she was picking out the cardboard. There's no reason to pretend anymore, and in fact I don't think it's possible for me to fake another smile to a person who's ruining my life.

"Why?" I say to her blankly. I drop the charade. My smile drops as well. All that's left is my rageful eyes that are nearly on the verge of tears. Her fake smile disappears as well, but she doesn't answer me. "Why are you doing this to me? What have I ever done to you?"

Stacy looks around the aisle and back at me, putting a hand on her chest. "Josie, what do you mean?"

I shake my head. "Why are you playing games, Stacy? The letters. I know it's you." I let out a nervous laugh. "That's why you're here. Stop playing games. Just be honest. Tell me the truth."

"Truth?" she says, surprised.

I can't stop the tears that've formed in my eye from falling freely now. "Why are you sending the letters? Why are you doing this to me? What have you done with my husband?"

"Kevin?" she says, looking down. I knew it. The way she says his name tells me everything I need to know. I can hear the regret in her voice. I glance behind her, and a woman is looking strangely at us. I imagine if I start screaming at Stacy, the cops will be called.

I don't care anymore. I don't care about anything.

When Stacy looks at me, I see a tear of her own. "I'm so sorry, Josie," she says softly. I look at her, confused. This was not how I imagined confronting her would be. I can feel the pain from her as another tear drops. "Kevin told me."

Now I'm the one who's utterly confused. Another woman joins us in the aisle, watching the show we're making.

Stacy clears her throat and wipes her tears. She lowers her head again. I knew that she was up to no good with my husband, but I never expected a woman having an affair with him to be so emotional when confronted by the wife.

She reaches out to me and holds me tightly. Confused and paralyzed, I open my mouth, but no words come out.

"I know about the baby you lost," she says. "I wasn't working with Kevin while it happened. He never told me. I have a sister who had a miscarriage. I don't know from personal experience but know from watching someone I love go through the same that it must have been the worst."

"I... uh." I struggle to find the words, and Stacy helps me.

"I feel so terrible for what I did," she says almost at a whisper.

When she says it so softly, I find my anger again.

This is a woman who's ruined my marriage. Either with the letters or by sleeping with him.

"I feel bad for calling you crazy at your house the other day," she says. "I know you heard me say it. I didn't understand why you were so upset. Now I get it. I'm so sorry." She looks at me endearingly. "I thought about reaching out to you to apologize but don't have your number."

I purse my lips. I have her number. I stole it from her Nexen profile at work. I don't dare say that though.

"If you ever need to talk," she says, "I'm a very good listener." She looks at the pink bunny. "We don't even have to talk about anything. We could get together and have a crocheting party."

I look at her, unsure what to say. I came here to discover what my husband's affair partner was doing, not to make a friend.

"I have to go," I say, utterly confused.

"It's okay, Jo," she says.

"I've got to go," I repeat. The two women behind Stacy are both putting on great acting performances themselves as they pretend to not watch the show. I put my hoodie over my head as if it has the power to make me invisible and hurry towards the exit.

When I look back, Stacy's watching me leave.

CHAPTER 34

That was not what I expected. I thought we'd make an entire scene, but not the empathetic type I just shared with someone I thought I truly hated. But I have to say, I'm surprised by how much she appeared to care.

Either she's the best actress I've ever seen, or she meant every word. She said her sister had a miscarriage. She crochets? I was too traumatized by her being nice for her words to fully sink in.

I'm not sure what I'm more surprised by. I wouldn't expect a woman who looks like Stacy to be into crocheting. I also didn't expect her hug to make me feel so... nice. This was a woman who for the past few weeks I imagined squeezing her head off like a dandelion.

I start to drive home, feeling defeated.

Mary wasn't home. Stacy—turns out she's a complete sweetheart.

Ugh. All I wanted was answers. Instead, I'm more confused.

Is Stacy pretending to be nice to me to throw me off? Is Mary missing because she's with my husband? Where is Kevin? When will he come home? Is my marriage completely over?

So many questions. My anxiety is through the roof. I'm half tempted to go back to the craft store and buy the pink bunny package. I do have Stacy's number obtained from work. Wouldn't it be nice to crochet and forget about all these terrible questions?

In two days, it's mine and Kevin's two-year anniversary. Will I be single before Saturday comes?

My life is not that simple. Somehow, I know all the questions I have won't be answered easily.

My life is burning to the ground, so I may as well make it worse.

Instead of turning down the street towards my house, I decide to make a quick detour. What happened to Amber the other day was my fault. I didn't report the letters to the police. I didn't do anything I should have. I let my curiosity control me. If I wasn't so stupid, maybe my friend wouldn't have been assaulted.

As I get closer to her house, I find some relief knowing this was one address I didn't have to illegally search at work. I've only been to her house once, months ago for tea after work. It was when we were first getting to know each other and a few days after she graduated training. It was a little awkward switching from being friendly at work to being friends in the real world. I'm glad we made it through that awkward transition.

It helped that Amber has the gift of gab. If I run out of things to say, I can always count on Amber to figure out how to continue a conversation. Her general temperament is cheery. A very positive woman. It was part of the reason I was happy to develop a friendship with her.

I can be a big downer with how I talk about myself sometimes. Amber is the opposite. Positive to a fault.

Maybe that's why not seeing her at work made today even more upsetting. Obviously, she wasn't there because of what happened to her.

I park on the street and look at her front door a few houses down.

I step out of my car and grab all the letters on the passenger seat. It's time I come clean to someone about what I've been hiding. I don't know how Amber will react to finding out that the anonymous person sending me letters is the one who attacked her.

I can't let that get in the way, though. She needs to know. I walk up her porch reluctantly, like a kid about to tell their parents about something they did wrong.

When I knock on her door, it doesn't take long for Amber to open the door with a smile. "Hey, Jo, what are you doing here?"

"Hi, Amber," I say. Her face is worse in person. I cringed at the picture she sent when I saw how black and blue her bruise was. The swelling in her face hasn't improved, but now she can see out of both eyes. "It's been a wild day. I wanted to talk to you. Are you okay though? Does it hurt?"

She slightly touches her face. "It looks worse than it feels." She opens the door fully. "Come on in. Do you want some tea or something?"

That was one thing I liked about her place when I first visited her. She had an upper cupboard full of different teas. I had never seen something like it before.

"I'll take matcha again if you have it," I say.

She gestures for me to sit in the living room as she goes to the kitchen. She turns on the tap, filling a kettle.

"Trey told me you left work today," she says. "I was going to text you to see if you're okay. So I'm glad you came."

The comment puts me back. I'm surprised that Trey

and her text each other. For a moment, I wonder if something is going on between them that I don't know about. They go to the bar together. Well, not alone on a date. They go together with a group of our colleagues. Still, though. They're both single. Both attractive. I didn't think Trey was Amber's type though. Trey has an old soul while Amber is much more vibrant. As they say though, opposites attract.

"Yeah," I say, "I left work early. That's part of the reason I came today. I have to tell you some things."

Amber looks at me from the kitchen with a playful face. "Oh, that doesn't sound good." She puts the kettle on the stove and sits on the couch across from me. "So, don't keep a girl waiting."

I take a deep breath. "Well, there's been more letters," I say, lowering my head. "I only told you about one, but since then, there's been three more."

"Really? I'm surprised you didn't say anything to me."

I nod. "I wanted to. I really did. But the letters warned me not to tell anyone. And even after things got worse, I didn't say anything because... I wanted to know the truth."

Amber looks at me, confused. "What are you saying, Jo?"

I take another deep breath. "One of the letters told me that Kevin was going to bring a girl home. It said he was cheating on me. When I was supposed to go to the bar that night, instead I parked my car blocks away and hid in my own house to see if whoever sent me the letter was telling the truth. And sure enough..."

"Kevin brought home a girl?" she says with a sickened face.

"Stacy Wingham," I say slowly. "Only when I confronted them, he said they were working late. They had binders of whatever in front of them, as they drank wine together." I shake my head. "Another letter said Kevin was having a date with a woman."

Amber shakes her head. "Jo, what's going on with you?"

I ignore her comment and frantically tell her the rest. "I went to the restaurant the letter said they'd be at, and I saw him with a woman, sort of. When I tried to see them together, he was sitting alone. I don't understand it at all. At first, I thought it was Mary, his ex-fiancée, doing this. You even said it yourself. She scratched my car in the past. She's a little unhinged." When I say the word, I have a weird smile, but Amber looks at me oddly.

I must be the one who looks unhinged to her right now.

"I even went to Mary's house today to confront her," I continue. "But she wasn't home. Next, I followed Stacy from her house. I don't think it's her, though. I—"

"Wait," Amber says, putting up a hand. "How did you even figure out where they live?"

I look at her, wide-eyed. "I sort of looked them up on our system at work."

Amber immediately covers her face. "Jo, what the heck are you doing?"

"You don't understand," I plead. "Amber, I need to know who's doing this to me. Whoever it is warned me not to tell others."

"Right," she says. "I wish you didn't tell me. This all seems insane. You can't be looking people up at—"

"I know," I say, cutting her off. "It was wrong. I'm already a few steps away from getting canned." I look at her bruised face. "It's because I told you about the letters that you were attacked."

"What?" she says, confused.

"The day my car was scratched, I found a letter as well. Whoever's doing this knows that you know. They may know about Trey as well. I'm not sure, but they definitely know that I told you about the letters. That's why you were targeted."

Amber looks at me wide-eyed, unable to speak. I thought maybe Amber would be upset when I shared the news with her. I didn't expect her to be her bubbly self, but her face right now is killing me. I can see the anger in her eyes. I can see the confusion.

"Why didn't you tell me about this sooner?" she says.

I lower my head. "Whoever's doing this knows the truth. Kevin hasn't even returned home. He texted me last night and said he was going to stay at a hotel. I'm not sure where he is or who he's with. He could still be out with the redhead I saw him with. I don't know. But whoever sent me the letter knows."

Amber looks pissed now. "So let me get this straight. You didn't tell me that I was attacked by your stalker freak, or whatever you have going on, because you wanted to find out more about what your husband is doing behind your back?"

When she puts it like that, I suddenly feel like the worst person in the world. It's the truth, though. It's exactly what I did.

"I'm so sorry, Amber," I say. "Look, I'm going to report this to the police. We can go together." I open my purse. When I do, one of the letters flops out onto her couch and I collect it quickly, taking the other three out. "I have the letters. We can go together. We'll tell them what happened to you. We need to figure out who's doing this!"

The kettle on the stove starts to whistle.

Amber doesn't respond. In fact, she's not even looking at me. Her eyes are glued to my purse and what's inside. Peeking out is the can of bear spray.

"That's just for protection," I blurt out.

Amber looks away, unable to meet my frantic gaze. "I don't know what to think right now. This is… a lot."

I zip up my purse as the kettle starts to shriek in the kitchen. "Amber, I never thought you'd get hurt. I'm—"

"I'd like you to leave," she says, cutting me off.

CHAPTER 35

When I open my front door, I could collapse to the floor immediately. What a day. What a rollercoaster ride. I likely complicated things at work. I actually used our system to track down my husband's ex-fiancée. I likely lost my best friend and apparently made a friend of a woman I assumed was having an affair with my husband.

When I step inside, it's pitch dark except for a little light coming from the kitchen. I'm surprised when the drapes are closed. I don't tend to shut them when I leave. I don't like the idea of Q being alone in the dark.

That's another thing. Where's Q? She's usually the first to greet me when I come home. She's like a giddy child happy to see me. That's something that makes Miss Q so unique from other cats I've had. Most of the ones before her kept to themselves, only coming out for temporary snuggle times. Not Q, though.

She's all about that constant attention. So, where is she?

"Q?" I say to the dark. My heart stops when I don't hear her. In my crazed state, did I not shut a door properly? Is she outside? Last time that happened, I spent the entire evening trying to find her.

From the kitchen, I hear her meow, and I let out an audible sigh. I close the front door behind me, and thankfully, Q brushes up against my leg.

"You wouldn't guess the day I had," I say to her, bending over to pick her up. I hold her close to my chest as she purrs. "Sorry I left you in the dark." I kiss her head as I cross the living room. I'm about to turn on the light when I hear a noise in the kitchen.

It sounded like a chair moving.

They're here. I know it. My heart sinks. "Hello!" I shout. "Who's there?" When I don't hear an answer, I drop Q.

Is this why Mary wasn't at her home today? She was at mine the whole time, waiting for me to return. I quickly unzip my purse and grab the bear spray. "I'm calling the cops!" I shout out, taking a step towards the kitchen.

That's when I see him. Kevin has a wide grin. "Suprise!" he says playfully.

I immediately hide the bear spray behind my back. "Kevin?" I say, confused. He's sitting at the kitchen table with several lit candles illuminating the large pot of pasta in the middle.

"Got home early," he says. "In fact, we're all done at work! We finished the project. I have next week off too. I'm giving the team some much needed time off. So I made us dinner," he says with a wide smile.

My mouth drops and I feel a tear welling in my eye. "I… don't know what to say. I didn't think you'd be coming home. I wasn't sure you would come back home, ever."

He lowers his head. "I know." He stands up from the chair and slowly wraps his arms around my waist. "I know it's been hard. I know these past few weeks have been hard on us. Now that work will be lighter, I can focus on what matters. You and me. I've had a lot of time to think about us."

"You have?" I say. I nestle my head on his shoulder. "I feel like I've been losing my mind. All I want is you, Kev. There's just so much going on. I don't know where to start."

Kevin takes a step back, a wry smile on his face. "Well, let's start with why you're holding a can of bear spray behind your back."

CHAPTER 36

He looks at me, confused, and I place the bear spray on the kitchen counter. "A lot's been happening," I say. "I haven't felt like myself."

"I know," he says softly. "I feel the same." He looks at the bear spray again. "Seriously, why did you have a can of bear spray?"

I take a deep breath and sit at the table. "It smells really good, Kev." I let his actions sink in. He finished the big project. No wonder Stacy came home earlier than expected. It makes sense now.

"Talk to me, Jo," he says, sitting across from me. "What's happening here?"

I let out a sigh. "I'm scared. I've been so scared, anxious... confused."

"Why?" he asks.

I glance at him. "I saw you the other day with a woman at Amore. You didn't see me?"

He looks at me strangely. "You were at the restaurant?"

I let out a nervous laugh, and he looks even more confused. I must come off like I'm completely psychotic given how I'm reacting. My husband gets off work early and surprises his wife with what looks like a delicious dinner, only to realize how crazy the woman he married is.

For a moment, I think about not telling him. I'd love to fill my plate with the lightly tomato-sauced carbs Kev made just for me. I'd rather enjoy the special meal. Afterwards, we could make love. Enjoy our anniversary this weekend. Instead, I'm going to ruin it all again.

I ignore his question. "Who was the girl you were with?"

He lets out a heavy sigh himself. "Jo, I don't want to fight with you. I have no clue what you're talking about. I went to that restaurant and ate alone. I went to the hotel alone. I'm not cheating on you. I've never cheated on you. I don't understand why you're like this!" He covers his face and slams the table. "I came home to make up with you!" I jump from my seat at his explosiveness. When he sees that he freaked me out, he softens his voice. "I don't understand why you've been so... well, like this lately. Why?"

I look down at my purse. Here we go, I think as I grab one of the letters. I place it on his empty plate. He reads the front and looks at me.

"What is this?" he asks.

"The first letter I received," I say, taking a deep breath.

"Read me now," Kev says as he examines the cut-out letters and heart shaped cardboard. He runs his finger along the side and opens it, looking at what it says inside. His eyes widen.

"That's how you knew about my work number," he says.

I reach down and grab the rest. "This one I found inside our house."

He reads the next and looks at me. "You never did

tell me why your car wasn't in the garage," he says, glancing at me and back at the letter.

"It's because I parked it blocks away. I hid in the closet upstairs and waited for you to bring home a woman."

He shakes his head as he snatches the third and fourth and reads them. "And the restaurant." He looks at me strangely. "I don't understand. Who would do this?"

I shake my head. "I don't know."

He looks over the letters, glancing at me several times. "Did you make these?" he asks, staring at me oddly.

"What?" I yell. "Of course not." I take a long breath.

"Who could be doing this?" he says, picking up one of the letters and looking inside again. "It's freaky."

"I thought maybe it was Stacy, or maybe Mary."

"My ex?" He shakes his head slowly. "Why would you think it's her?"

"I texted her that I'd call the cops about the letters and she replied that I'd find out what happened if I do," I answer. He looks at me oddly. "There's also my car. I found this letter on my windshield." I pluck out the one I found. "This letter was waiting for me after work, with a long scratch along my car."

"Someone keyed it?" he says, eyes wide.

"Worse," I say. "After this, and the letter saying I've been warned about not telling anybody, Amber was assaulted. I told her about the letter."

"Your friend from work was assaulted?"

"She doesn't know who did it. She was hit pretty hard."

He lowers his head. "I can't believe this."

I take out my cell and open Amber's message. "See? That's what they did to her."

He takes my cell and looks at the photo Amber sent me. He looks utterly shocked, lowering the phone in his hand. "This is... I don't know what to say. No wonder." He looks up at me. "That's why you've been acting this way. These letters. Why though?" He looks down at the picture of Amber, taking a deep breath, pursing his lips. "I'm so sorry, Jo."

"I must have come off like I was going crazy."

He lets out a heavy breath. "None of this is your fault." He shakes his head. "I thought this was all because of—well, you know, what happened. I didn't understand. I still don't understand."

I look at my husband and the wonderful meal he made for me. I think about the effort he put into all of it. Yet still part of me questions him. Is he telling me the truth?

A tear wells in my eye as I look at him. "Why would anybody do all of this?"

"I don't know," Kev says, wide eyed.

"I just want you to be honest," I say, reaching my hand out across the table. "That's all I ever wanted. The truth. I don't... I don't know what to believe anymore." I let out a sniffle as I wait for him to respond. "I just don't know. I want to believe you."

He lowers his head. "That's what love is," he says, reaching across and grabbing my hand, holding tightly. "It's you and me believing in it. I love you, Jo. I'd do anything for you. What we've been though together, nobody else has that on you. Why would I want anybody else?"

Tears fall freely now. "I know I'm not what you wanted. I gained weight. I let myself go. The diabetes. I'm a mess. A complete mess. Why would you ever want to stay with me? I don't deserve you. You're supposed to be with a gorgeous woman. Some girl like Stacy Wingham. Not me. I know you don't find me attractive anymore. Why would you? I don't even like myself." I wipe a tear from my face and look at him. He's staring right back at me. I can feel the disgust coming off of him when he looks at me. "You don't have to pretend. I know I ruined this."

Kevin lets go of my hand. After a moment, he stands up and comes closer to me. His hand grabs mine and he gestures for me to stand. He leans his head against mine, saying the most comforting words.

"I love you, Jo," he says. "You're the only one I love." He takes a deep breath, hugging me tighter. "I chose you because you're a good person. A good woman." He lets out a laugh. "You're truly the only good person I know. I mean that. I knew after a few dates that you were the one for me."

I cry into his shoulder, letting all my anxiety, self doubts and negative emotions out of me. "I should have told you," I say. "I shouldn't have let it get this far." I step back and look at his eyes. "I was scared that I was going to lose you."

He kisses me softly. "Never," he whispers.

"I let Amber get hurt."

Kevin takes a deep breath. "It's not good."

"What do we do?"

Kevin looks at me a moment, his face void of any emotion. "There's only one thing we can do." He reaches for his cell phone on the edge of the table. "Call the police."

CHAPTER 37

I already feel more like myself. I stare at my bedroom ceiling. When I turn, Kev is on his side, facing away from me. I thought my marriage was over. I thought Kevin was having an affair. I thought so many terrible things.

Kevin called the police immediately after I told him what was happening. He explained it to the operator. A police cruiser came to our house about an hour after we called. I was surprised by how long it took for them to arrive but one of the officers explained that as we weren't in immediate danger, the call was lower on their priority list.

The upside was I got to eat cold pasta with Kevin as we waited for the police. It wasn't the romantic dinner my husband planned for, but we made the best of it. He wanted to open a bottle of wine, but I reminded him that drinking before police officers arrived at our house was likely not a great idea.

I explained everything to the policemen. I told them about how I found each letter. I explained how one was found inside my house. How I believe my friend was assaulted because she knew about the letters. Police took down Amber's contact information. They said they'd reach out to her after they were finished at our house.

There was one awkward moment, though. A new

piece of information that caught Kevin by surprise.

One of the officers asked if anybody else knew about the letters. When I mentioned Trey's name, Kevin's eyes lit up and he turned his head to look at me. It wasn't me who told him exactly. Amber had more of a hand in that one. Still, me even mentioning Trey's name seems to bring out this jealousy in Kevin. I'd be lying if part of me didn't hate the idea that he gets jealous.

Makes me feel better about how crazy I've felt lately.

Before the officers left, they provided us with a case number. Kevin was not impressed. When he asked if that was it, the officers essentially said yes.

They advised us to think about getting a home security system. Nothing was taken from our house. We didn't know for sure if Amber's attack was related to the letters. One of the officers explained that the scratch on my car could have been what the letter was referring to. If we find another letter, we were told to call the police immediately.

When I explained that I was worried it was Kevin's ex-fiancée, Mary Halbec, who was behind the letters, they said they'd contact her as well and let us know if anything comes from it. Somehow, I know that nothing will.

When I said I also suspect it could be a woman named Stacy Wingham, Kevin gave me another awkward stare.

"She wouldn't do this, officers," he said, sticking up for his work wife. He didn't have a reason as to why it couldn't have been her. But Kevin pointed out that I don't have any evidence to support it being Stacy either.

The police officers left soon after. I felt like I was nowhere closer to finding out who's been messing with my head the past few weeks.

I look over at Kevin, laying in bed. Despite all the scary things happening in my life, I feel like I have my husband back by my side.

As if he could feel my gaze, he suddenly turns and looks at me. His soft eyes meet mine, and he caresses the side of my face.

"Whoever's sending these letters," he says, taking a deep breath, "is trying to ruin us." It's good to know I'm not the only one thinking about the letters. "That's the only reason I can see why they're sending the letters to you. They want us to turn against each other. They want to break us." He smiles at me. "That won't happen, though."

I smile back. "I know. I should have told you last week when I got the first letter." I shake my head.

He grabs my hand. "With everything that happened tonight, I didn't tell you my surprise. I wanted to tell you during dinner."

"Surprise?" I say, letting out a laugh. "What is it?"

He smirks at me. "Saturday's our anniversary. You didn't think I wasn't going to do something special for you, did you?"

I let out a deep breath. "I'm just happy we're here, in this bed together... But I like surprises. Do I get a hint about what it is?"

He laughs and moves closer to me under the sheets. He brushes his leg against mine. Soon after, he climbs on top of me and moves the hair from my face. "Maybe," he says, playfully biting my ear.

With each nibble, I feel my body aching for him. When I feel his manhood against me, I know he's thinking the same thing I am.

"I'll take this surprise anytime," I say with a smile.

He kisses my neck, and my body trembles.

"This is just foreplay to the surprise," he says playfully. "I booked us for the weekend at the cabin. Our special place."

He kisses my neck as a wave of ecstasy escapes me. "Perfect," I whimper. I was hoping he was going to tell me. I'm not in a state where I could handle any more surprises.

CHAPTER 38

I'm in my cubicle but today is different. I'm smiling and can't wait to get off work. Kevin's home today and next week as well. He told me he's going to get the car packed so that when I arrive home, we can just leave for the cabin.

In our first year when we went to the cabin, I felt how strong our connection was. I felt so loved. Mostly because we made love—and a lot of it. We barely took our hands off each other on our first-year anniversary at the cabin.

If last night is any indication of how the next few days will be, I know our second anniversary will be just as great. My heart flutters at the thought of it.

Plus, the cabin has all the amenities of what Kevin loves most in life, besides me. There's a large shed in the backyard with a canoe. There's hiking and fishing rods. A beautiful stream is only a short walk away. It's his oasis. With it being right on the lake, I love sitting outside with a good book.

Plus, it will be mostly just us in the area. The closest neighbor is a ten-minute drive away. Kev told me how the owner is a huge gun and hunting enthusiast. He gave Kev the code to his gun locker in case Kevin wanted to hunt and needed to store his weapons.

All I have to do, before having a much-needed dream weekend with my husband, is get through the rest of this workday. That's not as easy as it may sound. Already today, I've had two bad calls, and it's not even lunch time. The first man actually called me the C word. That one shocked me. I've heard plenty of bad words, but the C word is a first. The second bad call was much tamer but still frustrating.

Amber's at work today. I saw her this morning walking to her cubicle. I'm sure she knew that I was behind her, but she didn't look back to greet me. I wanted to say something to her but felt bad. Obviously, she's still upset. It may take some time to heal that wound.

I wanted to find out if the police went to her house to talk to her like they promised they would. Did they speak to Mary as well? I called the non-emergency police number and provided them with the case number earlier today. I was told there were no updates. The woman on the phone wasn't able to confirm or deny if the officers spoke to Amber or Mary. I requested a callback but was told it could take a day or two before they can provide one.

Perfect.

A stranger's been leaving anonymous and threatening letters at my house, and it feels like nothing is being done about it.

I went over the conversation I had with the officers yesterday in my mind. There's a chance the policemen are right. Amber's assault may not be related to the letter I found on my car. Isn't property damage enough of a consequence?

This weekend getaway is exactly what the doctor ordered. Not just for my sanity, but my marriage too. It's odd how quickly things can turn around. The other day,

I sat in my cubicle worried that my entire life was in flames. Today, everything feels like it's on track again.

I realized the stalker I have, the person sending me letters, doesn't control my life. They don't dictate what I do. I can't believe I played their games for as long as I did.

Kevin is quite concerned, though. In the morning, we had breakfast together. Actually, Kevin made me breakfast. Usually, he's the first out the door and last to come home. I could get used to having a lot more sex and eggs in the morning. Unfortunately, I know he will only have a week off from work before a new project will start. He tells me it won't be as hectic as the one he just finished.

Before I left for work, Kevin talked about getting a home security system like the officers recommended. I'm convinced that the person who wrote the letters didn't break into our house when they left the second letter. I must have left the back door unlocked. Kev and I don't have a key outside hidden under a rock or anything like that. There was no sign of forced entry.

The big, and only question, left is who's been doing this to me? Who's been doing this to us? It's easy to forget that the letters impacted Kevin just as much as me. It made me question our marriage. It brought our relationship to the edge.

I open a browser on my computer to look up the area Kevin and I will be staying. It's only a few hours away. We'll likely get there late tonight but we'll have plenty of time to enjoy our anniversary tomorrow. When the browser opens, several news articles pop up on the home screen. Apparently, a large bank stock has gone up twenty percent. There's an article on how eating more vegetables helps you lose weight that I consider clicking on. I'm about to type in the search bar, when the title of an article catches my attention.

"Another Calgary Woman Missing".

The bad news makes me hesitate a moment before I search the small towns Kev and I will be close to. I don't want to read about terrible things happening to others today.

This weekend is all I have on my mind. Kev loves spending as much time outside as possible when we go to the cabin. He's tried to talk me into hunting with him. I don't have a license, but as he tells me, in the back country, a license is not a big deal. He told me stories about how he, his dad and uncles would take shotguns out into the back country and fire at soda cans on rocks for fun.

Yeah, not my kind of fun. I do a lot to please my husband, but this time I'd like to go out to a restaurant at least once. Maybe Saturday we can go out for dinner on our actual anniversary. I found a high-ranked steak house thirty minutes away. Kev will balk at the time it takes to get there. Once he's at the cabin, he likes to stay near the property the entire time.

In a few more hours, I'll leave work and we'll be on our way to a glorious weekend. It would be nice if I could make up with Amber before leaving, though. If I can make up with my husband after everything that happened, there's a chance Amber and I can work things out too.

A red light on my computer starts to blink. I know what that means. It's my turn to take a call. I'm up in the queue for my next verbal beatdown from another customer. I can't. I just can't do it. My headset is already on my head, but I can't hit the connect button. The idea of it makes me physically ill.

I stand up from my chair, ignoring the call, and

step outside my cubicle. As I get closer to Amber's workstation, I look inside and see Trey. He's not working any harder. I see him reading the article about the missing woman. I knock on the metal frame of his cubicle but don't catch his attention.

"Trey," I say. He turns and smiles.

"Hey."

"Sorry about yesterday," I say. "I wasn't in a good headspace."

He nods. "Well, it's all understandable. If I got the letters you did, I'd be freaked out."

I smile. "Thanks for the coffee and the offer of a game of cribbage though."

"Still enough time in the day for us to play a round," he says with a smirk. "I'll try and be nice since you've been having a hard time lately."

I roll my eyes. "Things are better, though. I talked to Kev about everything. We reported the letters to the police."

He looks at me blankly for a moment. "That's probably for the best. What did the police say?"

I sigh. "I'm waiting for an update." I look at the crib board that's on his desk. "I'll be down for a game next week though."

"Now that you guys are made up, are you celebrating your anniversary?" He stares at me, waiting for a reply.

I'm surprised Trey even remembers things like this. "Yeah, going on a little retreat to this cabin. We went there last year too. It's nice." I look down the aisle towards Amber's cubicle. "I wanted to try and catch Amber before she leaves for the weekend."

He takes a moment to respond. "Amber took a mini break outside. She went for a walk."

I lower my head, defeated. I may not see her before the end of her shift. Amber likes going for walks on breaks, especially after a bad call. She says the movement helps get rid of the negative energies. Usually, she'd pull me aside to go with her, but not today.

I manage a thin smile. "Well, if you see her, can you let her know I came by?"

"Of course," he says with his own grin.

"See you next week," I say.

"See you," he says before turning his chair. When he does, a red flashing light appears on his monitor. He tilts his head to the side and sighs, reaching for his headset. I nearly laugh out loud at our shared misery as I head back to my cubicle.

I imagine I'll have another flashing light of my own waiting for me when I return. When I get close to my workspace, I realize what's waiting for me is much worse.

Mr. Dunstrow looks at me with an aura of discontent. "Josie," he says with a calm and stern voice, "I notice you're in the queue for a call but missed several call attempts."

I manage to put on a fake customer service greeting. "Happy Friday, Mr. Dunstrow. Sorry, I was just in the bathroom." It's a little white lie, but better than dealing with his wrath.

He shakes his head. "That's why I saw you in Trey's cubicle?" He lets out an audible sigh to ensure I know how upset he is. "Mrs. McNeil, you know that you're on a performance plan. Now is not the time to ignore your work. That's not what you're paid to do."

I take a deep breath. He's right, of course. "I'm sorr—" I catch myself before I finish the sentence. I've worked here for years. I've put up with the misery. I hate customer service. I hate putting up with the customers' abuse. I hate how much we charge for electricity. I'd be upset too! I hate how little support employees get from management like Mr. Dunstrow.

How many more years will I dedicate to a place that shows so little dedication to me?

"Josie," Mr. Dunstrow says, in his calm yet intense way. "Please return to your cubicle. I need to see that you're being active with the call volume we have. Like I said—"

I can't listen to another word from him. "I quit!" He looks at me, confused, so I help him understand. "I won't sit in that chair. I can't. I'm leaving right now, Mr. Dunstrow."

He watches me as if I'll change my mind. Taking out a small bin from under a lower cabinet, I fill it with a few of my things. He won't have enough time to call Tracy from security to walk me out at this pace.

CHAPTER 39

Work didn't go as planned.

It's odd. Today's the first day in a while where I felt happy. I was more present than ever, and maybe that's what made it nearly impossible to be physically at work.

As I drive home, it hits me: I'm unemployed.

Not exactly the best news to share with my husband before we start our relaxing weekend away. The upside is I'll be off work next week with Kevin. It will be nice to have more time together.

More than likely, it will hit me that I have no job and I'll start immediately looking. In fact, I imagine starting the search at the cabin.

I make a promise to myself that I won't let my explosive decision impact our time this weekend. Hopefully it doesn't ruin anything for Kevin either.

He won't be thrilled. He makes a good salary, though. We don't have much debt either, except the mortgage. I hope it won't take me too long to find employment.

I'm starting to realize that impulse-quitting probably wasn't the best idea, but I couldn't take it there anymore. At Nexen, most employees only last a few months. I managed to work years there. In retrospect, I should have quit a long time ago. There's going to be a transition period, but I'm sure I'll be okay.

I have a strong work ethic. I haven't been without a job since high school for longer than a few weeks. Nexen Power is the only employer I've ever rage quit. Plus, if I could put up with Mr. Dunstrow for as long as I did, I'm sure I can handle anything a new employer throws at me.

I sigh, thinking about Amber. If I text her, I'm sure we can talk about things. There's a lot of coworkers I'll miss. That's the only thing that kept me working at Nexen for so long.

The work was frustrating. Management was a pain in the rear. Although most customers that called were easy to work with, that ten percent of nasty calls made the job unbearable.

I think of Trey. No more playing cribbage at work. No more surprise coffees. I'll really miss that too. Kevin wouldn't be ecstatic if I planned time to see Trey.

But he does hang out with Stacy Wingham. After my last encounter with her, I'm finding myself liking her more. If Kev got to know Trey, there could be a friendship there.

I park in the garage when I arrive home. When I open the front door, I'm immediately greeted by the Missy Q. She nettles against my leg.

I pick her up immediately and kiss her furry face. "Looks like I'll be home a lot more for the next little bit," I say with a smile. "Can you help me find a job?" She looks up at me and I know she doesn't care about any of that. She just wants one thing. I start to pet under her chin and the side of her neck.

"Kev?" I call out. He doesn't respond. I wonder if he's upstairs until I realize his car wasn't in the garage. I figured he'd be packing his car, but he doesn't seem to be home.

I bring Q into the kitchen with me when I see it. A folded piece of paper is on the table. A piece of paper with my name written on the front in pen. My heart drops for a moment.

I sigh when I recognize Kev's handwriting. I feel stupid as I pick up the folded note to read it.

"Hey love," he wrote. "Grabbing some supplies. If you read this, I'll be back soon."

I smile as I place the note back on the table. Today truly is a backwards day. I quit my job. I made up with my husband. And even letters left for me don't seem so scary.

A knock on the door startles me. Suddenly, my thoughts of my life turning for the better are broken. I think of the anonymous letters. The last thing I want is to find another at my door. I glance at the kitchen counter where the expired can of bear spray sits. My thoughts start to spiral as the person outside knocks loudly.

How long will knocks and doorbell rings haunt me?

"Who's there?" I shout from the kitchen.

There's a pause. "Calgary Police, ma'am," the muffled voice of a woman answers. "Could you please answer the door?"

I let out a sigh and catch my running thoughts. I asked the officers for an update. I'm surprised I'm getting an in-person one. Maybe that's good news. Did they speak to Mary? Do they have more information about who's sending the letters?

I open the door, and a tall woman greets me. "Good afternoon," she says. I notice the gold shield on her belt and a holstered handgun. "I'm Detective Jennifer Calder. Are you Josie McNeil?"

I nod. "Yes, are you the detective assigned to our

case?" I ask. She looks at me, surprised. "About the letters?"

She shakes her head. "No, sorry. I'm here to speak to your husband. Is Kevin available?"

I look at her with my own surprised expression. "Uh, no. He stepped out."

"Do you know how long until he returns?"

I shake my head. "No, sorry." She purses her lips. "Can I give you his cell number?"

She smiles. "That's okay," she says. "I already have it."

Utterly confused, I ask the obvious question. "What's this about?"

"I've been assigned to a missing persons case," she says. "I'm hoping to track down those who were at one of the last spots where Ms. Susan Langwell was seen. We believe your husband was at the restaurant."

"Restaurant," I repeat. Immediately, I know which one. "You mean Amore?"

She looks at me, surprised. "Were you with your husband yesterday at the restaurant?"

What an odd question. "Well, I passed by it," I say. "I didn't eat with my husband, though. He told me he ate alone."

At least that's what he said to me. Suddenly, a whirlwind of thoughts swirl inside me. Thankfully, the detective settles them.

"That's what I was told too," she says. She opens up a notepad she removed from inside her suit jacket. She quickly looks at her notes. "Several staff members indicated that your husband ate alone. We're trying to figure out who Ms. Langwell was dining with as she wasn't alone. She was eating with an unidentified female."

While my thoughts about my husband settle, new concerning ones rise. "Do you have a picture?" I ask. "Of the missing woman? What was her name again?"

"Susan Langwell," the detective repeats. She takes out a photo from her pocket. "This is her." She extends her hand with the picture of the woman, but I don't take it. Instead, I stare at the pretty red-haired woman in the photo.

CHAPTER 40

When Kevin comes back home, he enters the house with a wide smile on his face. "You're home early! You just have to pack your bag and we are out of here!" When he doesn't see my shared enthusiasm, his grin disappears. "What?" He looks around the house. "Did you get another one? Another letter?"

I look away from him, not sure what to say or why I feel so emotional about it. "A detective came by the house. She wants to talk to you." I hand him a card Detective Calder left me before leaving. "Remember the night you were at Amore? There was a woman with red hair that you opened the door for when you got there."

He looks at me, confused. "I told you, Jo, I ate alone. Are you going to do this again? Why was a detective here?"

I shake my head. "The anonymous letter said you were there with a woman. I remember what she looked like. She had red hair. A young woman with freckles." He's still confused. I gesture for him to follow me into the living room where I show him exactly what I mean.

The sound on the television is muted. The reporter talks while seated, staring into the camera. An image of the missing girl is to his left. Beneath him is a rolling headline. "Foul play suspected in missing persons case."

Kev looks at me. "She was at the restaurant?"

I nod. "The detective wants to talk to you about her."

"Why?" he asks. "Do we need to go to the station or something?"

"She just asked that you call her," I say. I look at the image of the missing young woman, Susan Langwell. "I can't stop thinking about her. What if..." I look at him, just as confused. "The letters I got, what if it's related to her?"

"How?" he asks.

I shake my head. "I don't know. Nothing makes sense."

He kisses the side of my face. "Not everything is related to what you're going through with these letters."

I nod. It's true. There was a missing woman found dead last week. Now, a second has gone missing. I think of the young woman's face the night I was sneaking around outside Amore. The moment I saw her, I hated her guts because I assumed the worst. Now, the worst may have happened to her.

"I just hope they find her alive," I say. I think of the smile she had when Kev opened the door for her.

A young, pretty woman. It's a terrible reminder how scary the world is. The detective said she was sitting with another woman at the restaurant.

"I'm sure everything will be okay," he says, attempting to reassure me. Maybe I'm a pessimist, but I have a terrible feeling it won't be. Just like the other woman, I have this gut feeling she's no longer breathing.

The idea that I may be one of the few people who saw the young woman alive that night scares me. Her killer could have been at the restaurant. What if I saw her killer but didn't know it?

Kev flicks the detective's card in his hand. "Let's try and have some fun this weekend," he says. "I'll call this Detective—" He looks at the card. "—Calder. You get a bag ready. Let's leave the city and forget about all the things we're leaving behind."

I look at the television screen and the newsman's concerned demeanour. I can't stop staring at the young woman. Susan Langwell. I truly hope she's okay.

Kevin gives me a thin smile as he turns off the television. "Let's just go, Jo," he says. "What's wrong?"

I can't explain it. My thoughts run wild in my head. The past few days, I've been nothing but a mess. The anonymous letters. Me frantically trying to figure out the truth. The detective even explained that Kevin was confirmed to be eating alone. And yet there's this terrible feeling inside me that something isn't right.

"I told the detective about the letters," I say. "When she told me about the missing woman, part of me was worried."

Kevin looks at me and nods. "What did she say?"

"I gave her the case number. She'll look into it but isn't sure if it's related." I take a deep breath and look away from Kev.

I made the mistake before about not being open about what was happening. I kept the letters secret. Look what happened because of that.

He puts his hands on my shoulder and kisses my cheek. "Everything's okay, Jo," he says. "I know you're afraid. I'm freaked out too. Whoever's bothering us, we'll figure it out. We're going to get a security system soon. I'm off work all next week. I'll be home. Nothing will happen. If you want, I can drive you to work."

Him mentioning work that breaks me out of my

spell. I did say no more secrets.

"So," I say, trying to find the courage to tell him, "I quit today."

He takes a step back. "You quit your job? What happened?"

His glare at me makes me look away. "I couldn't handle that place anymore. The people I work with are great, but management, the job itself... it was too much. Most people quit after a few months. I was there for years."

He looks at me for a moment and smiles. "Well, looks like our vacation together will become a longer vacation when we come back."

"I'll start looking for work right away," I promise.

He waves me off. "Don't worry about that. Take a week off with me. We deserve it. Start looking when I go back to work." I smile and he kisses me softly. "Okay, so, how about you go pack that bag?"

I smile. "Fine."

"I'll call this lady and after that, let's hit the road."

I start to head up the stairs. As I do, Q follows behind me. Once upstairs, I grab a small case from the closet and unzip it. I open the bag, turn and look through the closet to pick out a few outfits. I want at least one sexy outfit for the steak house. I pick out a black dress that I know still fits me well. When I turn, Q is sitting cozily in the case. I sigh as I pick her up and toss her across the bed. That reminds me to bring a lint roller with me.

My cell buzzes and I answer it. To my surprise, Amber greets me.

"Hey," she says softly. "Trey said you came by to see me." She clears her throat. "I went out for a walk but wanted to call you."

I let out a sigh. "I was worried we wouldn't be able to talk." I sit on the edge of the bed. Q immediately starts to snuggle into me. "I'm so sorry about what happened to you. After I found the letter, I should have told you."

"I'm okay," she says. "I mean, it still hurts, but I called to let you know that you and I are okay. I know you've been going through a lot. The letters must have been scary. Not knowing what Kevin was doing. Him cheating on you."

"Well, we made up," I say.

I can hear her audibly sigh on the phone. "After everything you found out? ...I'm not trying to tell you what you should do, but aren't you worried you're being played again?"

"I don't think so," I say. "I even spoke to a detective about it. She confirmed Kev was eating alone at the restaurant I followed him to."

"Detective?" she says.

Ugh. When I think about what I'm about to say, it's hard to comprehend. I miss having a boring life. Netflix, pizza, snuggling with Q and sex with my husband. Sign me up for that type of life. This has been way too much excitement.

"Have you heard about the missing girl? Susan Langwell?" Amber says she's read the headline. "She was at the same restaurant the night I was following Kev. I received a letter telling me he was at Amore with another woman. So I checked it out myself. I actually saw Susan that night too."

What follows is an over-the-top, enthusiastic, "What!" from Amber. "This is all too much, Jo," she says.

"I know," I say. "I told the detective about the letters. She's going to talk to the other officers who came to our house last night. Kev doesn't think it's related." I sigh. "That reminds me, did you get a call from the police? They said they would reach out to you."

"They came by late last night. Scared the crap out of me."

"They didn't have any updates I guess?" I ask. Amber confirms they didn't give her any more information that I didn't already know about. "The police said they would contact Mary and Stacy too."

There's a pause on the phone. "And... any more letters?"

"None, thankfully," I say. "It's been a few days too. Now that I've called the cops, maybe I freaked them out."

Amber lets out a sigh of her own now. "So, you and Kev made up?"

I smile. "We did. He came back home. We're celebrating our anniversary by going to a cabin. We're about to leave, actually."

There's a pause before she says anything. "So long as you're happy, Jo, that's all I care about."

I've put my friends through a lot lately. Amber's been my shoulder to lean on through all of this.

"Have fun," she says. "I'll see you on Monday."

"Uh, you didn't hear?" I ask. I assumed everybody would have known about me quitting by now. I guess I wasn't loud enough with Mr. Dunstrow. "Well, I sort of quit."

Amber lets out a laugh. "Now I need details."

"The look on Mr. Dunstrow's face was priceless." I laugh too.

As I go over the juicy details, Kev walks into the room. He doesn't hide his discontent due to the lack of clothes in the case.

CHAPTER 41

The first two hours of the drive to the cabin are easy. As the road continues endlessly, our conversation starts to die down. Kev drives the whole way. I try to get him to switch with me, but he protests. He's always like that. He tells me I drive cautiously and says I have mild road rage.

I'd never heard of that term before. He explains that it's enough to curse to myself and get riled up at other drivers, but not enough to give one of them the finger.

I'm aware I'm not the best driver, but I'm not as bad as he jokes. But he says if he wants a fun date with me, him driving ensures I won't be so upset.

"So," he says glancing at me, "have you thought about what you want to do next for work?"

I sigh. "Not a clue."

"Customer service?"

I scoff. "Never again!"

We pass a sign on the highway and Kev hoots. "Not too far now!" He leans over and kisses my cheek. "I have to pee," he says nonchalantly.

I laugh. "Just pull over. You can technically do that anywhere."

He shakes his head. "What am I, an animal? I'm too bougie for that now. I require four walls to alleviate myself now. A room with potpourri."

I smack his shoulder. "What happened to my outdoors man? You don't just go outside when you're hunting?"

He smiles. "That's different. I'm in the presence of a lady at the moment. I need to give you the illusion that I'm not some beast."

After a few moments, Kev pulls off the highway down a dirt road. Gravel crunches under the tires as the tall trees on either side of the road close in, making the path narrower.

That's when I notice it. A car is parked on the side of the road close to a hiking trail. A red sports car. My eyes widen as I look outside my window.

I shake my head in disbelief at how my brain works. The car has a yellow thunderbolt along the side. The car I saw that night and the one in Mary's Facebook image didn't have a bright yellow thunderbolt. At least, I think so. I take out my phone and open up her profile again.

"What are you doing now?" Kev laughs. "Who cares what other people are doing with their lives on social media? Look where we are," he says, gesturing to the woods around him. "Let's be present."

"I am," I say as I click on Mary's profile. There's poor reception in the area and it's taking forever to load.

Kev laughs. "Okay, have your fun on your cell, but when we get to the cabin, we make a pact. No phones! No cells! Just us."

He glances at me as I frantically open the picture of Mary leaning on the hood of her car. It's hard to tell from the angle of the shot, but from what I can see, there's no visible lightning bolt along the sides.

"Deal?" Kev repeats.

I put my cell back in my pocket quickly. "Deal," I say

confidently.

CHAPTER 42

Kev pulls into the long, secluded driveway that leads to the cabin with a wide smile on his face. Surrounded by tall trees, he's completely in his element. The cabin is in the distance and beyond it is the sparkling lake that it rests next to.

"This place always gets to me," he says as he pulls up to the cabin. He's truly like a kid in a candy store. "Maybe we can squeak in a BBQ and some paddleboarding. What do you say?"

With the smile on his face, there's no way I could say no. Kev loves to BBQ, and I like to eat BBQ. That's a win for sure. I enjoy paddleboarding but with the day—no, the past two weeks—I've had, all I want to do is relax near the lake and read a good book.

That's when it hits me. I brought no book. Of course. Last minute packing and that's what I get. Kev rushed me. I hate it when he does that.

Last year when we came to the cabin, the landlord had a small collection of novels. Most were romance books with a half naked man on the cover. Not my genre. I was surprised, given how macho energy the rest of the cabin feels, that the books available were so corny.

"I'm game," I tell Kevin with a thumbs up. "BBQ it is."

"And paddleboarding," he says with a smirk.

He turns off the car and stares at me. When he doesn't say anything, I start to laugh. "What? Why are you looking at me like that?"

He shakes his head. "You promised," he says, reaching out his hand towards me. "Phone, please." I roll my eyes, but he doesn't seem impressed. "This is our two-year anniversary trip. An anniversary with your real husband, not your little minicomputer. This weekend is all about reconnecting with me, not connecting online."

I smile at his dumb joke and hand him my cell, which was already in my hand. "Good," he says, confidently. "Now we can have some real fun."

He gets out of the car, and before I follow him, I take in the beautiful views. Last time we came here, I would sit all day near the lake. I didn't much enjoy swimming in it. I only went once and it was ice cold, even in July. Kevin was upset that I didn't want to swim more, but I talked him into relaxing in the hot tub.

The idea of paddleboarding sounds too cold. I'll go in the water once, though, to make Kev happy. Marriage is all about give and take.

Kev's always the adventurer. I'm the relaxer. Which is why me not bringing a good book is extremely upsetting. Maybe when we go to the city for dinner tomorrow, we can find a store for me to buy one. There likely won't be a huge selection.

I'm not a picky girl. Any book by Freida McFadden or Stephen King would suffice and, thankfully, their novels are everywhere.

I step out of the car as Kev opens the trunk and takes out several suitcases and a bag out at once. I let out a laugh as he struggles to bring them all to the front door of the cabin. He awkwardly steps forward, leaning to one side as if he'll topple over. One of the bags slips from his hand.

That's Kev. The man has to try and take everything inside at once. He looks just as ridiculous when he brings in groceries at home.

"I'll get that one," I say, picking up the dropped bag. "I was thinking that tomorrow, for our anniversary dinner, we could try this steak house that's close by. Cattle Road Grill."

He looks at me, confused, as he waddles closer to the door. "Close?" he says with a tone. "Where close?"

"It's only twenty minutes away," I say. A little white lie doesn't hurt. If I said thirty, he'll resist more. I can see him make a face as he contemplates the gas mileage to get us there and back, despite us driving several hours to get here.

"Yeah, we could do that," he says. "But BBQ tonight and lunch tomorrow. I bought a couple of steaks for tonight," he says, making a weary face. "I didn't know you wanted steak twice, sorry. So long as you lie and tell me my steak is better, I have no concerns with a fancy date tomorrow."

"Deal," I say.

I take in the rustic beauty of the cabin itself as Kev reaches for the front door, nearly dropping a suitcase on his foot. He makes a face as he opens the door. As we step inside, it takes me back to last year when we were here for our first anniversary.

Not much has changed in a year, of course. The kitchen takes up a small corner near the back door. Copper colored pots and pans hang close to an antique gas stove. It's a gorgeous kitchen for a small cabin. Although there is one development that's new. A piece of paper is taped to the dishwasher. "Out of Order," someone wrote in pen. Ugh. If there's anything I hate more, it's washing all of my dishes. Kev notices it and laughs.

"You wash and I dry," he says.

"No deal," I say playfully.

The living room is small but cozy, dominated by a stone fireplace that takes up much of the wall. The bulky, old fashioned television set makes it clear the landlord isn't glued to the screen. Next to the couch is a shelf with a small collection of books. I immediately smile when I notice there's a few non-romance books to choose from. Some even look like thrillers, my favorite genre to read.

Beside the shelf is the gun locker. Another fun outdoor activity Kev enjoys. It's not my thing either, but part of me is glad it's here.

Last year, we invited the elderly couple that lives down the road, Henry and Laura Besmit, for lunch outside near the lake. Henry told us a story about how the year before he saw a massive grizzly right near our cabin. The idea of that scared me enough to move my outdoor reading activities inside for the rest of the stay, with the door locked. Kev mocked me, explaining it's the animals' land.

I realize that's what else we forgot. Bear spray. The can we had is expired, though.

As much as I enjoy coming to the cabin, our next anniversary will be at an all-inclusive beach resort where the worst that can happen is food poisoning.

I'm about to look at what books the landlord has when I notice Kev struggling with the bags. "Sorry," I say, running up to him. "I'll take this one to our room." I grab my case and take it to one of the small rooms.

By the time I'm back in the living room, Kev has

managed to bring in the cooler from the car. "I'll unload that too," I say. Kev thanks me and goes back to the car to get the rest. He loaded up that backseat in the car with anything he could. It will take him some time, and when I'm done, I'll help put away everything else.

I open the cooler and start taking out some of the food items and placing them in the fridge. An egg cracked on the trip up here. I throw out the broken egg, but some of it lands on the floor. I sigh as I grab a paper towel and attempt to wipe it up. Half-frozen egg residue from the ice in the cooler on genuine wood floors. Great.

Kev enters the cabin. For once, his smile is absent and he genuinely looks upset.

"What's wrong?" I ask.

He shakes his head. "I can't believe I forgot to buy some." He lets out an angry sigh. "Wood. I didn't buy any. The landlord always tells me to bring some. I checked the back, but they don't have any."

I want to remind him that's what happens when we rush getting ready, but don't.

"No big deal," I say. "I'll pan fry the steak."

He purses his lips. "We're only here a few nights," he says. "We have to enjoy a fire by the lake tonight. It's tradition." He looks at the cooler. "I won't go to town. It's too far. How about I go visit Henry and Laura down the road? They'll have some wood, at least what we need for tonight. Tomorrow, we can grab some more in town."

"Sounds good," I say, standing up. "It would be nice to see them again."

I do truly enjoy seeing them. If ever there's a future couple I would aspire to be like, it's the Besmits. With the wrinkle placement on the older couple, you can tell they've had a lot of enjoyment in their lives, full of bright smiles and loving times. They may be older now, but I feel they were a beautiful couple when they were younger. They had five children together, and nearly ten grandchildren. Last year, Laura mentioned another was on the way. I'm sure she'll show me all the photos of their newest grandchild when I see them. That's a lot of kids and grandkids. A feat that makes me a little self conscious.

I'd be happy with just one child.

All of their children are older now, of course. Henry and Laura only summer at their cabin and have a condo in the city when the snow comes, which feels like it's nearly every month of the year in Alberta.

"That's okay," Kevin says. "Stay here. If you unpack, we'll be able to enjoy the rest of the day more."

He smiles at me. Some day, I hope we'll be an old happy couple like Henry and Laura. Sitting outside, enjoying each other's company until dusk.

It would be nice if I could talk Kev into playing cards with me, but he hates most games. I find it more enjoyable when we don't play games against each other. He hates losing. He's a mild sore loser.

"Okay," I say. "Well, say hi to them for me. And let them know they should come over again for lunch. Maybe we can have them come by Sunday."

"Good idea," Kev says. He comes up and kisses me softly. "I'll be back soon."

He places my cell phone on the kitchen counter and puts his in his pocket.

"What happened to no phones?" I ask.

"Here's not the place to be stranded on the road without one," he reminds me with a smile.

CHAPTER 43

I finish unloading things from the cooler. I'm about to start setting up the table inside when I look out the window and take in the view of the shimmering lake. A picnic table is by the small private beach area.

Dinner outside seems much more romantic.

I bring some plates out with silverware on top. When I go back inside, I'll start dicing up some onions, cherry tomatoes and salad for a side dish to Kev's steak. It won't take too long for him to cook them up. Instead of putting away those groceries from the cooler, I left them out and grabbed a kitchen knife along with a cutting board. I made sure we had what we needed for dinner in case I needed to call Kev to raid more from the Besmits' house.

When I'm at the picnic table, in horror, I notice several cobwebs.

I make a face. I'm such a city girl. It's not that being in a cabin doesn't have its charm; I'm just used to everything being more sanitary.

Last year, on our first anniversary, I loved being here. I'm not sure if it's because I just love being around my husband or the scenery, though.

We've been through so much the past year with the miscarriage and with what's happened the past two weeks. I'm just happy to be back at the cabin again with my husband. Just a day ago, I thought my marriage was completely over. I look around the cozy cabin. And now, I'm here.

I hope this trip is just as relaxing and amazing as our first-year anniversary. Things will get tough in marriage. I know we'll have our ups and downs. All couples do. So long as we don't give up on each other, we can make it through anything.

I take another moment to enjoy the view of the lake, before placing the dishes down. I head back inside to start chopping what I need for the side salad, but the knife isn't there.

I'm half in a daze, realizing I'm not paying attention. Maybe it's the views. I notice a roll of paper towels and grab it. I'll need backup to take care of those ancient cobwebs outside.

I'm still annoyed about the knife though. The landlord only had one large knife for cutting. Where did I put it? My mouth opens when I see my cell phone on the floor. The screen is cracked.

Perfect. I let out a sigh as I pick it up from the floor. Just as I feared, it's not turning on. How did I manage to break my cell? Did I knock it off the counter?

When I turn my head, I get the worst surprise of them all. Red paper is sticking out from behind the sink. My eyes widen when I see the heart-shaped letter with familiar cut-out words on the front.

"Read me now!"

Here? They're here? I pick up the letter, unable to stop myself. Part of me wants to run and scream out the door and into the woods. Kev took the car with him. He'll be back soon. I just have to stay safe until then.

Despite me knowing I shouldn't, I open the letter. I can't help it. I need to know what it says.

The cut-out letters mock me as I read its message. "Happy Anniversary."

I feel frozen. Paralyzed with fear. They knew I'd be here. But how?

"I've been waiting for this for a long time," a soft voice says behind me. When I turn, a familiar face grins at me, a knife gripped in their hand.

CHAPTER 44

"Amber?" I say, confused. She doesn't answer. She continues to smile wickedly as she takes a step towards me, the tip of the knife in her hand pointed at my face.

Before I can say another word, she slashes through the air towards me. I shout and step back, but the knife catches the end of my wrist. As my skin peels open, I shout again, still holding the paper towel. Instinctively, I grab a hanging pot and toss one at her. It hits her chest, and she shouts at me, lunging towards me.

I'm faster though and manage to open the back door. I run towards the lake, realizing as I do the fatal mistake I've made. There's no escape at the waterfront. When I look back, Amber's too close to get to the woods. All I have is the table between me and her. Thankfully, I've given myself a few weapons for myself.

I pick up the steak knives and pocket one, gripping the other in my hand. As she gets closer, I grab one of the plates and whip it at her. I completely miss. As she nears me, I go around the table. She follows me and we circle the picnic table. I grab the second plate, this time feeling more confident about my accuracy at such a close range.

"What are you doing, Amber?" I shout, the reality still not hitting me. "The letters were you? Why?"

The wicked smile disappears for a moment. "What

we had was special," she hisses. "He loves me, not you."

"Kevin?"

"You idiot!" she shouts, knocking the handle of the knife on her head. Her bruised face and intense eyes send a ripple of fear down my spine. "I told you he was cheating! You didn't listen. I told you about the second phone. You didn't listen. You never listen! You're too stupid to see what was right in front of you." She tries to get closer. I move around the table, holding the much smaller knife in my hand, the plate in the other.

"He was supposed to leave you," she says. "He promised me. Then you get pregnant and he changes his mind? How like Kevin, am I right? Well, that wasn't good enough for me. You were supposed to be out of the picture. So, because he wouldn't do it, I thought I'd give you a little nudge in the right direction." She lets out a sigh. "Do you know how many times I could have just killed you? The only reason I didn't was because of him. Because he loves you. How could he love you?"

She screams as she runs towards me. I try my best to use the table to keep a distance, but I know she'll catch up soon. I raise the last plate in my hand and smash it down towards her. This time it strikes her shoulder, cutting her upper arm. Amber shrieks and stares at me, eyes full of rage.

"You!" she shouts, seeing her cut skin. "Look what you've done!"

"Amber, just stop!" I plead.

She doesn't stop. She won't. I can see it in her eyes. She's going to kill me. Behind me is the house. I just need to get inside and lock the door and I'll be safe. I glance back to measure the distance. When my eyes meet Amber's, I know she realizes what I want to do.

I run as fast as possible to the back door. I don't look back. I know she's behind me, knife in hand. Without seeing her, I imagine the knife right over my head, with Amber ready to strike me as soon as she's in reach.

I make it to the back door, but as I shut it, Amber throws out her other hand. When I slam the door, it strikes her arm and she screams again. The door bounces back as she steps inside the house. Her one arm appears broken from the force of it. She doesn't seem to be in pain as she holds the long knife in the other hand and approaches me.

Cornered, all I can do is fight.

Suddenly, she stops. She lowers the knife and looks behind me. When I do the same, Kevin is standing in the living room. A rifle's in his hand. He's holding it at his shoulder, looking down the barrel.

I don't understand why he's pointing it at me.

"Kill her!" Amber shouts.

Kevin glances at her and squints at me.

"No, Kev!" I shout.

But it's too late. Kevin pulls the trigger.

CHAPTER 45

My body tenses until I realize what's happened. I wasn't hit.

When I open my eyes, Kevin is still holding the rifle, only the barrel is pointing towards the floor. I look down and see what's left of Amber's lifeless face staring up at me. Her life's blood pools below her body in the kitchen.

"Are you okay?" Kevin says.

All I can do is look at the woman I thought was my friend. My mind is still trying to rationalize what just happened.

"It was her," I say, still dazed. Kevin doesn't reply. I repeat myself as if saying the words again will help me make sense of it all. I look up at Kevin. "She says you two —"

When I look at Kevin, he purses his lips and shuffles the gun in his hand. "What did she tell you?"

I look at him, amazed. "That you two are together."

He shakes his head. "We were together. It happened a long time ago."

"She said you were going to leave me," I say, still piecing it together. "So that you could be with her."

"That's not true, Jo." When I meet his eyes, a chill runs down my spine. "None of it is true."

"You cheated on me," I say.

He lowers his head. "I did," he says softly. "A long time ago." He looks down at Amber's body. "She was crazy. It was a stupid fling. One night after we fought, I made a mistake. We hooked up. I could tell she was nuts. She tried to get me to leave you. I told her I wouldn't. We had just lost our baby. I wasn't thinking straight. We were fighting a lot back then."

"It was more than once," I say.

He shakes his head and takes a step towards me. "No, I'm telling the truth."

"You knew it was her sending the letters, didn't you?" I take a step back, looking down at the blood touching the edge of my white sneaker. I quickly get out of its path.

He looks at me sternly. "I thought it might be. I didn't know the Amber you worked with was the Amber I..." He looks down at her corpse. "I didn't know any of this would happen. How could I?"

I catch my breath, my adrenaline starting to slow. "Call the police," I say to him. I suddenly feel a sting of pain from my arm. When I look, blood is dripping from the open wound where she cut me.

"You believe me, though," Kev says, taking another step towards me. I look at him. His soft eyes are locked on mine, but he shuffles the rifle to his other arm.

"Kev," I plead, "please, call the police."

He notices my gaze on the weapon. He takes a deep breath and places it gently on the kitchen table, pulling out his phone.

CHAPTER 46

Police and an ambulance arrived within thirty minutes. Those felt like the longest minutes of my life. Kevin placed the rifle back in the gun locker after he called 911.

EMS arrived first. A paramedic looked at my arm. I was told it was deep but wouldn't require stitches. The wound looked worse than it actually was.

The police bring us separately to a nearby police station. I find it amusing that as we went to a nearby town, we drove past Cattle Road Grill.

My thoughts race the entire trip to the police station. It was Amber. I can't believe it. I trained her myself at Nexen.

Amber said she had wanted to kill me for a long time. Although, I can't remember all the terrible things she said at the cabin. It's all one bad dream that I somehow survived. But she made it seem like she had attempted to kill me before. I was at her house. We had tea.

How many times had we talked in each other's cubicles? How many lunch dates did we have?

The black eye. Did she do that to herself? She actually took that rock and struck her own face?

Kev was right. She was nuts.

And my husband, who's in the police cruiser behind me, lied to me. How many lies has he told? He said it was just a one-night stand. A one-night affair he had after we lost our child. How can I trust what he says, though?

How can I trust anything he says?

I sit in the back of the police cruiser. I feel like I'm being arrested. What will the police say when I tell them my story? Who will they believe?

How many more lies will Kev tell?

Kev is asked to wait in the hallway as police question me first. I tell them everything. I tell them about the letters, Amber's self-inflicted injury. I explain how Kevin saved me at the cabin using the landlord's rifle.

When they're done, I'm brought back to the waiting area. To my surprise, Kevin isn't there. They must have taken him to another room to talk already.

I sit in a chair and look at the clock in the room. It's getting late. But part of me doesn't want to leave the station. I feel safer here.

I have a sudden pain in my arm and know the Advil the paramedic gave me before we left is starting to wear off.

Amber. Amber?

As I sit alone, I put more pieces together. Amber started working at Nexen Power to get closer to me. How long was she planning on hurting me? Why didn't she just kill me? She had the opportunity to, likely many times.

On our walks at work, sometimes we would go on secluded trails nearby. How many times could she have murdered me and left me in a wooded area? How many times had she thought about murdering me?

She could have done it at any time. Had she felt she

225

got too close to do it? What stopped her?

I think about Detective Calder from Calgary Police. She said that the missing woman, Susan Langwell, was dining at Amore with another woman.

Could it have been Amber? I don't understand.

A police officer enters the waiting room. "There's a motel in town," he says with his gritty voice. "If you want, I can drop you off."

"How long will they be speaking with Kevin for?" I ask.

He purses his lips. "They have a lot more questions for your husband. Plus, not to mention, he killed someone in self-defence with a rifle. That's a crime here."

I lower my head as more pieces of the puzzle start to fit. "I need to make a phone call."

CHAPTER 47

I sit in my living room, reunited with Q. I didn't wait for Kev to finish being questioned by the police. As the officer told me in the waiting room, he'd be some time before he was released.

Our anniversary trip ended almost as soon as it started. I can't help but think about Amber. I have so many questions with very few answers. It's why I haven't been able to rest since returning home.

My mind has been spinning with so many dark thoughts. My closest friend was having an affair with my husband and plotted to kill me. My husband lied. I know now it wasn't the first time. I have the proof I need now.

But it hurts. I find myself second-guessing everything I'm doing and everything I will do.

Initially, I wanted to believe what Kev told me at the cabin. He's so good at being believable. That's when I worked out what I feel happened. And it's much worse than I ever thought.

There's only one thing I need now. I need my husband to admit to it. I need the truth. I need his lips to open and for once, just once, tell me what really happened.

I can't help but wonder how long I've been under his spell for. How many other women were there? How many times did I blindly trust my husband?

I got a text message from Kevin a few hours ago, saying that he was driving back home. Any moment he'd be entering our house.

The worst part is that it's well past midnight. It's officially our anniversary.

I hate myself for not leaving immediately. I should have never come back to this house. I could have taken Q and took off. I hate myself for needing to do this with Kevin. It's almost like an intervention for liars.

I pet Q softly. She looks up at me lovingly, and I scratch her under her chin. "I'm stupid for believing everything he said, aren't I?"

I'm stupid for thinking he'd offer up the truth. I should be long gone from this house. If I had any sense, I would be. Instead, I pet my cat and wait for my husband to return.

Finally, I hear the garage door slowly open. It feels like it takes forever for Kev to open the front door. When he does, he immediately lowers his head when he sees me. He looks back up, his face full of emotion, but his eyes are dry.

"I was scared you wouldn't be here," he says. "You never texted or called back."

I stand up and Q jumps off my lap. "It's been a hard night."

He looks at me softly. "I need you to know, I'm sorry. What happened with Amber was just—"

"I know it wasn't though," I say, cutting him off. "You two were together for some time and were still together when you killed her." I won't let him continue to gaslight me any longer.

"Jo," he pleads. "Listen, I—"

"I saw her in the video," I say. "She was at Amore with you that night." His eyes widen. "When Amber sent me the letter that you were at Amore with a date, I immediately got to the restaurant in time to see you enter with the missing woman. I thought she was your date. She wasn't, though. I took out my cell to record you inside the restaurant. I hoped I'd catch you cheating. Instead, you were sitting alone. But, when I looked at the video I recorded, I saw her. Amber. She was sitting at a table near you. Across from her was the young woman with red hair."

Kev looks at me surprised. "I can ex—"

I cut him off again. "It was Amber who texted you last week. She was the one who you 'had fun' with. It was her, wasn't it?"

Kev doesn't answer this time or feed me more lies. All his tales are catching up with him now. I still need him to admit to it.

"What did you do with her that was so much 'fun'?" I ask.

He glances at me and looks at the door. I imagine him wishing he could bolt through it and run away from this conversation. It's not that easy, though. He's stuck here with me, and I need the truth.

"And," I continue, "if Amber was sending me the letters, telling me to go to Amore, why would she do that knowing she was the one sitting with a woman who's now missing? Why would you be in the same restaurant, sitting near your lover as she dined with Susan Langwell?"

Kevin's face darkens as he looks at me. "Stop, Jo," he pleads. "Just stop this."

"It wasn't just about sex with Amber, was it?" I

continue. "This was something else. The text message from last week wasn't about just sex either. Soon after, the body of that other missing woman was found."

Kev scoffs. "First, I'm a cheater, and now I'm a killer, Josie? Is that what you're implying?"

"All I want is the truth, Kev," I say. A tear forms in my eye as the thought of what I've been through plays in my mind. "I deserve it. Please. I'm your wife." Kev lowers his head, looking away from me. "You chose me, though," I say. "Tonight, at the cabin, you could have killed me. It was what Amber wanted, wasn't it? But you didn't. I love you, Kev."

When he looks at me, his eyes are wet now. "I never wanted to hurt you, Jo. You were going to be the mother of my children. It wasn't your fault what happened. It wasn't your fault that she didn't make it. You don't understand. How could you? You are such a good woman, Josie. That's why I wanted you. That's why I have you. But I know what I am. That's why we lost her. It was God's way of punishing me for the things I do. I never blamed you. I blamed myself. I thought I could right the wrongs with our child. But because of my sins, it didn't happen."

Tears run down my face. "You killed those women with Amber. Say it. Say it for me. I need to know the truth now. A good marriage needs to be based on truth. So, tell me."

Kev takes a deep breath. "When I met Amber, I knew she was just like me. We connected almost immediately. We hunted together. We found our prey as a team. Sometimes I was the decoy, to lure in the target. Other times, it was her. It wasn't always sexual, I promise that." He looks away again. "After the miscarriage, she wanted to kill you. I wouldn't allow it. I never would. I never knew she became your coworker. I never knew she was sending you the letters. It was just like I said in bed with you last night. Whoever was doing this was trying to break us up. Trying to pit us against each other."

I let out a heavy breath. "You only knew when I showed you the picture of Amber's bruised face?"

He nods. "That's right. She was trying to manipulate me. She was trying to put you in a position where I'd allow you to die. That's when I knew the right decision to make. That was to choose you. And I always will."

"Kev, the things you've done. I—"

"That's over now, Jo," he says. "I mean it. This worked out perfectly. Amber will be solely blamed for the missing women... and the others."

I lower my head. "I don't know who you are, Kevin. You're not the person I thought you were. You're not the man I married."

He takes a step towards me and cracks his knuckles. "I told you the truth, Jo. Besides Amber, you're the only one who knows who I am. That was why I was still with a woman like Amber, because she could accept me. Accept what I do. You... were always too good for a person like me. I never was going to hurt you. I suppose I've been lying to myself this whole time."

He takes another step, and my eyes widen, knowing what he's planning. I wanted the truth. I needed him to say it, and now that he has, it's time for me to drop the charade.

"Help!" I shout, not remembering the code word I was given.

"It's too late," Kevin says, a wicked smile on his face. "I love you, Josie." He raises his arms towards my face.

A loud crash at the door stops him in his tracks

as a SWAT team storms inside. Detective Calder follows behind them.

Kevin, realizing what's happened, lowers his arms slowly. He turns and his eyes harden as he gazes at mine. "Well played, love. Well played."

Officers grab him forcefully, placing him easily in handcuffs. They tug at him, gesturing towards the front door.

Detective Calder comes up to me. "I have a social worker on scene for you to talk to, Josie," she says softly. "I listened to everything you said. I know that wasn't easy."

I smile, tears still rolling down my cheek. "I finally got the truth," I say.

Kevin grunts and yells at the officer to not be so rough.

"Kev!" I shout at him, my stern voice even catching the arresting officers by surprise. Kevin looks at me and his face softens as our eyes meet. For a moment, I see the man I thought I married. "I want a divorce."

CHAPTER 48

Three years later

I watch the much older man plant his lips on the pretty young blond woman. I'm a fair distance away but cringe at the idea of his scraggily mustache touching the lips of another. I couldn't handle that. I'd barf right on him; in fact, my stomach feels a little queasy. But now's not the time to mess up. I'm on the job.

I use my lens, aim and shoot. Taking several photos, I sit back in my car and look at the digital results. These are the photos that make it all worth it.

Satisfied that my work is done, I roll down the car window and allow some fresh air. It's truly a lovely night. Not too hot. A nice summer night.

The perfect night to go for a stroll along the riverside after a fancy meal at a local restaurant. A beautiful way to end a date night. I can see why the young woman, whose name is Tiffany, would consider kissing the nearly geriatric Charles Montclaire.

There's one big problem that's ruining the gold-digging romance blossoming in front of me. Tiffany is not Charles's wife.

Charles's wife, Sandra, is the one who hired me to see if her husband of over forty years has been cheating on her. The photos tonight are enough to prove what she'll need.

Tiffany is Charles's secretary. He's a wealthy man in his sixties while Tiffany is only twenty-five. How very cliche. How disgusting.

But my work on this case will help Sandra move on. Charles won't be able to gaslight her into believing his lies any longer. The proof I'll give Sandra Montclaire is all she'll need to embrace the next chapter of her life.

Divorce.

It's a difficult chapter, no matter how amicable the two parties are. The Montclaires have adult children, so I'm sure that makes divorce a little less complicated. The problem for Charles is the very large amount of wealth he accumulated that he'll have to split with Sandra. I imagine she's in for one large settlement.

Another satisfied customer.

Sometimes I think about my old career at Nexen. I still miss the people who I worked with. I had a good group of work friends. Some I'm still in close contact with. In fact, one I see every day.

I take out my cell and dial his number. Trey picks up right away. "Hey," he says. "How's the stakeout going?"

"Much better than I hoped," I say. "I got what I need, so I'll be coming home early."

"I know what that means," he says playfully. I roll my eyes at his sensual tone. "Netflix and snacks!" He laughs.

After what happened, it took some time for me to find peace again. Trey and I didn't start dating for more than a year. Fast forward and our two-year anniversary from when we got together is coming up in a few months. How time flies.

I was obviously a complete wreck after finding out

my husband was not only having an affair but was also part of a serial killer duo. Every couple has their thing. Some play board games together, like Trey and I, others murder.

Being with Trey has opened my eyes to what a relationship can be like. I used to think I had to be heads over heels to be with a man. He had to be drop dead gorgeous. He had to check all these boxes on my list. Many of them were very superficial.

I had a mix of complex emotions after finding out about Kev's affair with Amber. He picked a woman younger and more attractive than me. Oddly, it helped me realize how superficial I was being in my relationship with Kevin.

I didn't give Trey the time of day because he didn't get me excited in the same way Kevin did. But I overlooked the best qualities that make Trey and me so different from anything I've had before. We trust each other. We have many things in common and the same morals. We love spending time together.

Kevin and I had very little in common. Even my attraction to him seemed one-sided, given what he was doing behind my back. But he and Amber have a lot more in common than I did with him. They shared a dark interest in murder.

They found the body of his ex-fiancée, Mary, in the trunk of her red car parked in the garage at her house. It was determined that someone had used her car for some time after Mary was killed. Kevin blamed Amber for the murder. He said she was jealous and killed his ex without his knowledge. He claimed Amber was using Mary's car.

That made sense. I saw the red sports car near my house one night.

Realizing I'm letting my thoughts run away from me, I try to stay in the present. "What are you up to?" I ask Trey.

"Not much," he says. "Hanging out with Missy Q." I can hear the faint sounds of her loud purrs.

"I'll be home soon," I tell him.

"Love you," he says. I smile and say the same back as we end the call.

I look out at the night sky and the beautiful full moon. Charles and his secretary are still kissing, which is putting a damper on the mood. I turn the ignition.

Tomorrow, I'll finish the paperwork and inform Sandra about my findings. As sad as she'll be, I know this is what she needs. It's what drove me insane all those years ago.

Looking back, how Kevin gaslighted me hurt me deeply. The way he played with my mind cut the deepest. I truly felt I was going insane.

It's one of the reasons I became a private investigator. It's hard to gaslight someone when you have proof that's irrefutable. That's what Sandra will receive.

I remember that terrible day when I confronted Kevin, the night he was arrested. He had told me I wasn't so good at sneaking around. I wasn't good at discovering the truth.

Well, turns out he was very wrong. It's a lot easier to blend into the background when the people you're following don't know who you are.

When I was trying to discover the truth about who was sending the letters and what Kevin was doing behind my back, I found it exciting in a weird way. That was another reason why I decided to be a PI.

Plus, if all works out well, I'll never have a boss like

Mr. Dunstrow again. I'm my own boss now, and I have to admit I'm very nice to my employees, which is just me.

The publicity around what Kevin and Amber did helped me have a new career. The media loved the idea that I became a private investigator, helping others discover infidelity in their relationships. It boosted my newly started business straight from the get-go. I took advantage of a bad situation and gave it a positive spin.

Kevin's situation only got worse though. Life in prison without the possibility of parole. At least that was his initial sentencing. Now, he's attempting to get a better deal. For years, Kevin used his lies to make the best life he could. Now he's using the truth to his advantage.

What a complete psychopath.

He and Amber murdered more than a few women. There were more that nobody knew about. Who knows how many people Kevin killed before I met him.

The night he was arrested, he knew he was doomed when he found out our conversation was being recorded. He pled guilty in an attempt to get a better sentencing deal. It didn't pan out that way. Life in prison. But now he's telling authorities where some of the victims are buried. He's hoping this will help reduce his sentence. While the families of his victims are happy to find some closure, it's hard to see him ever reaching freedom again.

Many times, I blamed myself for him and Amber's crimes. How did I not know I was married to a serial killer? Trey actually went out of his way to make a list of married serial killers where their spouse had no clue about their secret double life. I was surprised by the number of murderers he found.

Only, Kevin didn't live his double life alone. He had his partner in crime, Amber.

It took a lot of time to heal from those wounds. I'm much better now. I rarely think of him or Amber these days. My poor eating habits are better controlled and my gestational diabetes resolved itself. My sugar levels are now normal.

Sometimes when I'm with Trey, though, it's hard to not think about how drastically different my life is now.

It took a long time, but part of my journey after ending my marriage with Kevin was finding a way to be kind to myself. When I was able to do that, opening myself up to others was much easier. Trey was patiently waiting for me to be ready.

When I wanted love in my life again, I found it in one of my best friends. But before Trey, I discovered how much love I had for myself.

EPILOGUE

Two years later

I lie in bed staring at the ceiling.

Taking a deep breath, I raise my left hand and look at my wedding ring. It's been over six months since Trey and I married. I glance at my husband, who's breathing hard and sleeping on his side, facing the wall.

Who would have thought me and him would be in the same bed, married? All those years ago, we met at Nexen Power. We hated the job but enjoyed being around each other. Our friendship developed and flourished. I always knew Trey was a good person.

I knew being with him was what I deserved. Sometimes you have a sixth sense about who you know you should date, and who you should stay away from. When it came to Kevin, it was fairly easy to look past his red flags because of how handsome he was. Sometimes how attractive we are can hide the ugliness inside. That was truly the case with Kevin.

Trey is the complete opposite. A man who authentically cares for me. We're kind to each other.

I've come to think of marriage as a plant. No one intends to kill a plant when they buy it. They want it to grow. They want it to last forever. They don't want to replace the plant.

Ongoing maintenance is what's required to help your plant grow. You need to water it, give it sunlight as needed. Sometimes you forget about the plant but remind yourself how much you like it and give it more attention.

Although, when it comes to psychopaths like Kevin, I suppose some people do think about murdering their plants. But this analogy works better for regular people.

Trey and I work well together as man and wife. We give each other attention. There are times we get a little complacent, but when that happens, one of us surprises the other with something. A fun date, or a weekend getaway, or something a little spicier in the bedroom.

Who would have thought a game like cribbage could be so naughty? We still love playing together, but one night Trey had a fun idea. We'd play a game of cribbage with the muggins rule in full effect. Only, instead of gaining points that your opponent didn't count right, you'd be forced to lose a piece of clothing.

I'm much better at counting points in cribbage than Trey is. For a change, Trey doesn't mind when we play cribbage with muggins now.

I smile and stare at Trey's back. The idea of our naughty games makes me consider waking him from his slumber with a fun surprise. I'm thinking the plant needs watering.

But before that can happen, I need to take care of something. I slip out of the bedsheets and clumsily head towards the bathroom in the dark. As I pass my slumbering husband, a light illuminates the room. It's coming from Trey's cell that's on the nightstand beside him. A text pops up on his screen.

It's a little late for a message, I think. I can't help myself. Curious, I look at what it says. My heart sinks when I read the words.

"Love you. Call me. It's been a while since we talked." Beside the message is a kissing face emoji. Immediately, a flood of emotions hit me.

My eyes widen when I see who the message is from. Mom's cell.

I let out a heavy sigh and start to laugh. Trey moves in the bed, opens one eye and looks up at me. "What are you doing, Josie?"

I smile and sit on the mattress, giving him a long sensual kiss. "I love you, Trey."

❊ ❊ ❊

Note from the author:

I truly hope you enjoyed reading my story as much as I did creating it. As an indie author, what you think of my book is all I care about.

If you enjoyed my story, please take a moment to leave your review on Amazon. It would mean the world to me.

Thank you for reading, and I hope you join me next time.

Sincerely,
James

Download My Free Book

If you would like to receive a FREE copy of my psychological thriller, The Affair, email me at jamescaineauthor@gmail.com.

I'm always happy to hear from readers.

Thanks again,
James

Now, please enjoy a sample of my book, Lie Lie Truth:

PROLOGUE

"Tell me about your father." I can hear the audible sound of the camera behind the interviewer zooming on my face. The host of the popular show *Crime Pod* waits for my response to his open-ended question.

Where do I even begin?

A member of the recording crew shuffles the light. I suppose the lighting isn't right for the dramatic answer that the crew hopes will come from my lips.

Instead, I look away, unsure why I even agreed to be here to begin with. I've avoided interviews my entire life. I've never gotten into true crime, because I lived it. Why put myself through the trauma of the terrible lives others have gone through when my own is difficult enough?

The host, Chris Harrelson, lets out an over-the-top sigh, staring at the producer behind him. I can almost read his mind: "Make her say something. Anything."

The producer, an empathetic woman named Heather sitting in the dark with the rest of the crew, looks at me. Her facial features soften as she sees how upset I am. I didn't even realize a tear's been running down my face. I quickly wipe it and put on a fake smile.

"Sorry," I say to Heather. "I'm okay. We can keep going."

"Are you sure?" she asks.

The host abruptly stares at his wristwatch and back at the producer.

"If you need another break, Ali, you can have it," Heather says.

"I'm fine," I say. I remind myself why I'm here. I never wanted to tell my story before. But it's important. What happened when I was a little girl in the small town of Kadestill is infamous.

What happened to my father was talked about around the world and in criminology classes across the country. I've been pestered for years to speak about it, and it wasn't until now that I agreed to.

Every true crime fanatic knows the name Dennis Kempmen. His life and death are talked about more now than ever after what happened when I returned to Kadestill.

The host waves over a woman who did my makeup and asks her to touch up an area on his neck. His impatient face brightens momentarily before it goes back to its normal look of being mildly irritated. I can't help but smile when I see the change in his behaviour.

It's part of the reason I'm here.

I remember the conversation I had with my brother, Jason, so clearly it's as if it just happened. The host perfectly defines what Jason and I spoke about.

The masks we wear. The true selves we hide from others. This host does a wonderful job when the cameras are rolling to portray himself in a different light.

The producer gives me a wry smile, and I again give her confidence that I'm ready by offering a shy thumbs up. The host shoos away the makeup artist without thanking her as the crew begins filming again.

Chris Harrelson's bleak face softens immediately, expertly portraying sympathy for the camera.

"Tell me about your father," he repeats.

Again, I can hear the camera that's aimed at me zoom in closer. Taking a deep breath, I can see Dennis, the man I called Father, in my head. I remember the day he brought me to his house, after him and my mother, Connie, adopted me. I can see me, the scared little girl wondering what my life was going to be like with these two strangers.

"Where do you want me to start?" I ask the host.

"Wherever you want," he says. "We want to know your story. What was it like living with Dennis Kempmen? What was living in the town of Kadestill during the Red Ribbon Disappearances like? How did you feel when you found out your father was the main suspect? Tell us what happened when you returned to Kadestill over a decade later." The host clears his throat and takes a sip of water. His actions make me uneasy, and I try to find the words to respond.

The host leans in, his face somehow softening more.

"Are you okay, Ali?" he asks softly. At first, I'm surprised that he seems so human towards me, until I realize the cameras are still rolling.

I nod. "I am."

The host leans back. "Did you always believe your father was a serial killer?"

CHAPTER 1

Before

The woman named Connie Kempmen, who I would soon call Mother, sits in the front passenger seat of the car, as my new father, Dennis, drives.

The two share a smile as Connie looks at the back seat, at me, her new daughter. When I look past Connie's endearing smile, I see Dennis giving me a similar look in the rearview mirror. His grin grows wider as we share a quick moment.

My new brother, Jason, sits on the other side of the back of the car, looking outside the window. He's wearing a white cap backwards and looks more than bored from the long drive from Calgary to Kadestill. We haven't spoken much to each other besides him telling me his name.

It all seemed surreal. Dennis and Connie Kempmen dressed nice. Dennis wore a pair of khaki pants with a button-up white shirt. His short hair was combed perfectly. His face was cleanshaven, except for the pencil-thin mustache he had. His aftershave stunk up the car, but I wouldn't dare ask to lower the window to not suffocate from the smell. Every so often, he'd fix the dark framed glasses on his nose as he drove.

Connie had on a flowing white summer dress. Her smile was so infectious that even I felt compelled to give my own. There was an awkwardness in the air. None of us really knew what to say to each other yet.

They didn't know, but I was terrified. Today, I had a new family. I was adopted. But what if they were like the biological mother and father I was taken from? Dad had gone back to prison. I never knew why, but Mom told me he'd be gone for a while this time. I'd be a teenager by the time he was able to come back, and that was if he was on his best behaviour.

I was okay with that, to be honest. Dad liked to yell. Dad liked to shout. Sometimes, when I didn't listen, he'd do more than bark.

He was the complete opposite of my new dad. Dennis Kempmen had nothing but a large smile on his face the day he picked me up in Calgary.

After my dad went to prison, my mom said she couldn't care for me on her own. It was too much, she claimed. I found out later that it wasn't exactly her preference. The province decided to remove me from her due to the "unsafe environment," as they defined it.

Mom would typically heat up leftover pizza for lunch, but the day I was taken, there was no food in the fridge. A knock on our apartment door changed my life. A child worker asked if we could talk outside while a police officer spoke to my mother.

That was the last time I saw her. At the age of eleven,

my entire life changed.

"Do you like horses, Allison?" Connie asks me. She turns and looks at me again, her smile beaming as she waits for my response.

"Kind of," I say.

She nods. "Perfect. Just perfect. The Draysons, friends of ours in town, have two at their house. They live on a farm outside Kadestill. They give free riding lessons. Isn't that right, Jason?"

Jason looks away from the car window and matches his mother's gaze. When he doesn't respond, Connie rolls her eyes. He gets the hint.

"Yeah, it's cool," Jason says. He immediately looks back outside the window.

Connie smiles again as she looks at me. "Well, we'll take you to their farm someday soon. You'll love it."

"Thanks, Connie," I say.

"Mommy," Connie corrects me. "You can call me Mommy, or Mom." My new father, Dennis, turns to her and the two share another quick look. "Or whatever, Allison. Whatever you like."

"Call me Ali," I say to her. "My friends at school call me Ali."

I see Dennis look at me in the rearview mirror again. The wrinkles around his eyes make his smile seem more genuine. "Okay, Ali. I know this is a change for you. You can call us Dennis and Connie, if you want. Whatever you're comfortable with." I nod, and he looks back at me and his son. "Jason calls me butthead sometimes, but I'd prefer something nicer."

His son laughs, and Dennis's laughter booms over him. I can't help but do the same.

Dennis pulls off the highway soon after. Minutes later, we pass a sign. "Welcome to Kadestill. Population: One hundred and fifty."

I smile, thinking I must have read the sign wrong. How can there be a town with so few residents? The farmlands that we've been driving past become more wooded as we enter the small town. The trees stand tall, their branches swaying gently with the wind, casting long shadows across the paved road. We drive by a group of small buildings. One of the larger ones is a general store. Beside it is an ice cream place that's shaped like a giant cone with strawberry ice cream on top.

"Do you like ice cream, dear?" Connie asks, pointing towards the small shack. A few kids are lined up outside it.

"She's not an alien, Mom," Jason answers for me. I smirk at his joke and look at my new mother, who seems slightly hurt. I quickly wipe the smile from my face. I know what happens when little girls give attitude to adults all too well.

"Chocolate is my favorite," I say promptly.

Her smile reappears. "Mine too," she says. "Maybe we can go soon." She exchanges another look with Dennis and back at me. "I bought you some clothes. A few dresses, to start school with. But maybe we can ditch the boys and go shopping in the city soon. Just you and I.

Would that be nice, Ali?"

I smile again, wondering what's happening to me. When I was taken from my home in Calgary, I was told I wouldn't be seeing my real mom again. That I would need new parents. I was nervous. What if I had a new mom and dad who didn't like me? Or what if they were mean? Bad people. I'd have to go to another home.

The Kempmens seemed normal. The type of families I always imagined only characters in the cartoons I watched had. The type that wasn't real.

Jason looks at me. He's been unusually quiet the entire car ride from the city but now brandishes a smile of his own. "There's this awesome flavor at the ice cream store Tiger Twist. You have to try it. Crazy good, but sour."

"I like sour too," I say.

I watch my new family with amazement. They all seem to be happy. All are smiling. I don't think I ever saw my real dad brandish one for more than a few seconds. These people have them permanently etched on their faces, except for Jason.

I watch as my new father turns down a cul-de-sac. He's smiling to himself as he parks in a driveway.

I look up at what feels like a mansion. It's two storeys, with a brick finish and white siding. A white fence stretches across what looks like a large backyard. There're only six other houses on the small street. Each looks just as cozy. A large field sits between our house and the one beside us.

"Welcome home, Ali," Dennis says as turns he off the

car and removes his key. Connie opens my door for me as I step onto the driveway, still confused that this is the new life I have. My guard is still up though. It all seems so nice. Perfect. Too good to be true. A reality that a young girl like me is not supposed to have.

"Welcome to the Kempmen family, dear," my new mom says. She wraps her arms around me and squeezes a little too tightly. Dennis gives her a weird facial expression.

He lowers himself to one knee and stares at me, fixing his dark-rimmed glasses. "We made a room for you," he says. "It's your bedroom, so you can change it however you like, okay?"

I'm not sure how I look, but Dennis's smile wanes. He wipes a tear from my face that I didn't know was there and gives a thin smile.

"Should we go inside?" Connie asks excitedly. "Do you want to see your new home, dear?" Dennis purses his lips as he stands up and pats me on the shoulder. "Go ahead," Connie says. "Open the door."

Dennis nods at me as I take a few steps up the cement porch. When I open the door, the room is dark. I see silhouettes of dark figures in the back of the room. I'm confused until the light turns on and an eruption of people shout "Surprise!" at me.

There must be over twenty people there. Some are holding balloons. A few kids with whistles in their mouths blow as loud as they can.

A man with a grey flat cap in his hand walks up to me. "Welcome to the family, Allison!" he says. A woman in a red dress stands beside him with her own wide smile.

"Ali," Dennis corrects him. "Call her Ali, George."

The man named George nods. "Ali," he repeats. "I'm your Uncle George." He points at the woman in the red dress. "This is your Aunt Sandra."

I say hi to them both as Dennis laughs. "Don't worry about forgetting my brother's name. He's not that important." George shakes his head in response.

I look around the room filled with people. Most are neighbors. One man in particular stands out in the crowd. A man in a police uniform. The cop smiles at me as he catches my gaze on his police badge.

Dennis puts his hand lightly on my shoulder as I take in all the friendly expressions and warm greetings from what must be half the town of Kadestill.

What I didn't know in that moment was that the people in this room would be responsible for the worst night of my life.

CHAPTER 2

Present

Eighteen years later.

I sit across from the human resources lady who's plastered a wide smile on her face. "Thanks for meeting with me, Ali," she says with a soft voice. "How's your day?"

"Thanks, Karen," I say, my expression matching hers. Typically, nobody would be happy to have HR ask them to come to their office for a private meeting straight after entering the building, but today is different. Karen Swalding can only be wanting to meet with me for one reason.

I applied for the promotion to director of services a month ago and had three separate interviews. There's only one other person in the office who's had the same amount of interest for this position with the same number of interviews

Cassandra Wilton. She's a nice woman, but I don't think she's a good fit to be the top person of a non-profit organization that serves struggling families. She's very robotic with her care. She does her job as expected and is not a bad worker, but there's no heart in what she does. People aren't metrics. Our responses to the needs of the families we work with are of the utmost importance in what we do. We need to be available for them. She doesn't exactly respond back with quality.

Like her, I care about their requests for a call back if we're not immediately available. The difference between me and Cassandra, though, is that I come back with something of substance. I give them answers, sometimes ones they may not like, but I give them promptly with alternative solutions.

"Well," Karen says, looking down at her blank notepad, "I wanted to see you regarding the director position."

I'm not sure if it's the sudden break from her smile to a bleak stare or her looking away momentarily, but the positive energy that Karen tends to exude changes quickly. You can almost taste the tension now. I'm always bad at faking expressions when I'm nervous.

I know this isn't going to go the way I want and try my best to not show it. I'm likely failing miserably though.

"We've decided to go with a different applicant for the position," she says, her eyes softening on mine as she gives the crushing news.

I'm shocked. I've worked for Families First, one of the largest non-profits helping struggling families in the Toronto area, for nearly ten years. Cassandra has been employed for less than three. Everyone at Families First comes to me with their questions. Not just the families we serve but all of the employees. When the current director had to take some time off work after a sudden divorce, I stepped up for several months until they returned to work. Cassandra wasn't asked to run the non-profit back then, and it was only last year. When the director resigned from their position for a new one, it was almost a given that the job was mine.

I'm the only family resource worker who meets with their families in person. Most of us work remotely now, but I always make an effort to go to the office when I can, especially when I organize meetings with families. Most of the other workers, including Cassandra, do their work over the phone or by email.

I go to where they live and meet them for our first meeting. I like to understand their needs and them as individual people. I can name you every single family member of the over twenty families I work for currently, including their pets.

How many could Cassandra name?

She's not a terrible worker, but her heart is not in the work. It's all about the metrics. Qualitative evidence of her work and not the work itself.

It suddenly hits me that this is what matters to the non-profit I work for. Our mission statement says: "Families First. Where What Families Need Comes First." If you were to show the outcomes of the families I worked with compared to Cassandra's, hands down this competition would be won by me.

Instead of explaining this to Karen, showing her

why she's making a mistake by not hiring me for the top position, I nod. "Can I ask why?" I ask.

Karen's smile wanes again until she finds her confidence. "We love the work you do here, Ali. We do. It's felt that Cassandra is what we need to move the public profile better."

I bite my lip as it all sinks in. They hired Cassandra as director not just because of her perfect metrics. She also looks good on paper and in person. She's always wearing her pantsuits and looked like an executive before getting the job. Me, I wear jeans and a t-shirt because it comes off more approachable with the people I work for. Cassandra is exactly the type of face a non-profit wants to show why more funding is needed to continue to grow our outcomes.

But I'm a major contributor as to why those families are happy with our services to begin with.

Karen takes a deep breath. "Plus, we know you're going through a lot right now. It's probably better that you focus on family."

I can't help but shake my head in disgust. Because I've taken some recent days off to tend to the people I care for in their moments of need, that makes me unfit for the head position?

Suddenly, another realization hits me. Our grant money from the city and province are nearly finished. New grants and propositions to politicians, philanthropists and organizations will be needed. So they want to put their best robot in front to help.

"Families First. Where What Families Need Comes

First."

I nearly want to puke at the thought of how insincere the statement is. Money is what matters most to these people, not a leader who takes the work we do seriously. Who passionately does everything they can to help the families who need it.

The fakeness of Families First, a non-profit I've put a decade into, strikes me like a slap across the face. Looking at the fake smile on Karen's face is making me even more annoyed.

"I understand," I say. I stand up, indicating that I'm ready to leave. No reason to stay in this room.

"I was hoping to offer you a new position, though," Karen says. "We want to make you the team lead of family resource workers."

In the ten years I've been here, we've never had such a position. All of us have our caseloads and answer directly to the director.

"It's a position we want to make for you, Ali," Karen says.

I turn to her. "What would I be doing in this position?"

Karen nods and smiles. "Well, the rest of the team would come to you with their questions or concerns, and you would assist them as needed. You'd maintain and keep a caseload of families as well. You'd still meet with Cassandra together as a team. The position comes with a two-thousand-dollar pay increase."

I almost scoff in response, but even I'm surprised at

how well I don't immediately react. Basically, I'd be doing the same thing I am now but with a small pay increase.

"Can I think about this?" I ask.

Karen seems surprised by me not immediately accepting the offer. "Of course."

I shake her hand before leaving her office and head back towards my cubicle. Along the way, I pass a few colleagues chatting to each other. One of them is Cassandra herself. The new soon-to-be-announced director of Families First. For a moment, we share a glance, before I turn my head.

I know I shouldn't be angry at her. Who wouldn't want a promotion? I just think she's not the right person.

My cell buzzes in my jeans. I take it out and almost scoff again when I see who it is.

"So, did you get the job?" he asks. I don't know why I even answered the phone. All his voice does is irritate me. Realizing how stupid I am for giving him any time of day, I hang up immediately without saying a word.

I put my cell back in my pocket. He has no right to ask. He has no right to be a part of my life anymore. I've told him so, and yet here he is still calling me.

No, I didn't get the job. Yes, my life feels like a mess right now. A big part of that is because of you!

And no, Karen, I don't want to take on a role doing something I'm already doing. It's almost like they're going to pay me two thousand more a year, thinking that will make me content.

My problem, though, is I love what I do. There are others like me who work here who care for the clients we serve. We actually make a difference. Cassandra getting hired as the director means that this non-profit is going in the wrong direction, in my opinion.

It will be more about metrics. Call backs. Paperwork. Bureaucracy. Doing things to check a list and not because of the purpose we're here for.

It's so frustrating. My cell buzzes again several times in my pocket. He's calling again. Great. As if my day wasn't hard enough. I have to tell this man to leave me alone again!

I take my phone out and remind myself not to shout into the receiver while at the office. My mood changes when I see a different name on my cell screen. Jason Kempmen.

A ping of grief hits me. Is this the call I've been fearing? Is this how I find out?

"Jason," I say, answering the phone. "Is everything okay?"

There's an audible pause before he answers. "Mom's getting worse."

Made in United States
Cleveland, OH
23 September 2025